THE POUNAMU PROPHECY

The Pounamu Prophecy

© Cindy Williams 2015
Published by Rhiza Press
Copyright 2015
Cover design by Production Works
Photocredits: istockphoto, Arena Williams by Hemi Williams.

ISBN: 978-1-925139-45-7
National Library of Australia Cataloguing-in-Publication entry

Creator:	Williams, Cindy, author.
Title:	The Pounamu prophecy / Cindy Williams.
ISBN:	9781925139457 (paperback)
Subjects:	Ngati Whatua (New Zealand people)--Fiction.
	Prophecies--Fiction.
Dewey Number:	A823.4

The POUNAMU PROPHECY

A sweeping story of love, betrayal and hope

CINDY WILLIAMS

rhiza press
rhizapress.com.au

Ha aha te hau e wawa ra, e wawa ra?
He tiu, he raki, he tiu, he raki
Nana i a mai te puputarakihi ki uta
E tikina atu e au te kotiu
Koia te Pou Whakairo ka tu ki Waitemata
Ka tu ki Waitemata i oku wairangitanga
E tu nei, e tu nei!

What is this wind that blows
Rattling around me,
'Tis the north wind
Bringing the nautilus shells ashore
Bringing a new people, new ideas, a new order.
There is another wind I feel rising from the south, a cold wind
The carved post rises on the shores of the Waitemata
A symbol of authority and power (beware of it)
Good will eventually come to Tamaki Makaurau
Ah ... my vision is that of peace.

Prophecy Of Titahi, Ngati Whatua Tribe, 1780

AUTHOR'S NOTE (DISCLAIMER)

Although parts of this novel are based on historical events, I have portrayed them as I imagined them, not as they actually happened. All the characters in this novel are inventions with the following exceptions:

Judge Acheson, a Native Land Court judge and avid supporter of the Maori people.

The Commissioner of Crown Lands and the Chief of Police. I have taken their speeches directly from the original footage in the film documenting day 507 on Bastion Point: Bastion Point – The Untold Story www.nzonscreen.com/title/bastion-point-the -untold-story-1999.

The Minister for the Treaty of Waitangi Negotiations. I have taken his speech directly from the New Zealand Government website: www.beehive.govt.nz/release/deed-settlement-signed-ngati-whatua-orakei.

There was indeed a 'pistol packing preacher', Reverend Thomas Herangi, and I have taken a portion of his speech from Sharon Hawke's book: Takaparawhau – The People's Story: 1998 Bastion Point 20 Year Commemoration Book (Moko Productions, 1998).

I have also taken two other quotes from this book: the young man who says he has 'never been so blessed in his life' and the quote from Joe Hawke: 'What have we got to lose...'

There was a 'precious little girl' who died on Bastion Point and I would like to acknowledge her parents and the grief that surely never leaves them.

The Bible verses are from the NIV translation. In order they are: Romans 12:19-20, Jeremiah 29:11, 2Timothy1:7, Proverbs 6:27, Psalm 32:3-5, Isaiah 6:6-7, Matthew 6:9, Isaiah 40:31, John 15:13

Other sources consulted:

Peep through the Ponga: Ngati Whatua o Orakei, Their Story by J Neville Salisbury 2009.

www.terabyte.co.nz, www.teara.gov.nz, www.ngatiwhatuaorakei.com

ACKNOWLEDGMENTS

I would especially like to thank Grant Hawke, Chair of Ngati Whatua o Orakei Maori Trust Board, for generously giving up his time to tell me the history of the Ngati Whatua tribe. Some of these memories were clearly painful to recount and I greatly appreciate your strength and patience in answering the questions of an unknown Pakeha girl.

Thank you also to my father-in-law, Haare Williams, for your expert guidance on Maori culture and language, and your enthusiasm and willingness to share these riches with not just me but also your children and grandchildren.

To my husband, Hemi. Thank you for working so hard so I didn't have to.

To James. Always take pride in your rich cultural heritage – Irish, Scottish, English and Maori. And never forget that 'someone' is always looking after you.

1

I ran towards the burning whare – straggly hair sticking to the tears running down my cheeks. 'Teddy, Teddy! I forgot Teddy!' Wooden walls caved in, a sheet metal roof crashed to the ground. The fire was hungry and fast. It devoured our village while the government men stood by, their pale faces pleased with a job well done.

'It's too late, mokopuna.' Granddad stepped into my path and caught me up in strong, wiry arms. A tear rolled down his tough brown cheek. He smeared it away with his tattooed forearm. He stood firm, legs planted on his land, arms wrapped around me. I cried for my home, for Teddy and for Koro because he wasn't meant to cry.

'Crying is for sissies,' Rewiti always told me. My brother was a few years older than me – about eight or nine and boy could he punch hard. Whenever we had a fight I would run away and hide in the bush where only the tuis and Teddy could see my tears. Now from the safety of Koro's arms I saw Rewiti and his mates darting between the collapsed, smouldering whare, stuffing lumps of melted metal into their pockets. They would make great sinkers. I knew. That's all those boys did: swim and fish.

'You kids stay away! Get back to the beach where it's safe!' Dad's face was black from smoke. He was coughing and panting for air as he struggled to keep my Nanny from marching back to her burning whare.

'Mum, you've got to come. No good you dying in there. Do what you've always told me to do: Stand up and fight. Don't let them beat you.'

'No son. My time has passed. It's your time now. My place is in my home, on my land. When it goes, I go.'

The men had to carry all the kuia up the hill. They refused to walk.

But we walked. We walked up to our new houses that the government had built for us – with new stoves, new fridges, new everything. Mum said it would be good. Dad was dead against it – 'Boot Hill' he called it.

'They're stealing our land and booting us into shoddy state houses. How long do you think they'll stay nice? What about in a few years' time when the fridge packs up and the paint starts peeling off the walls? What then? Houses fall down but land lasts forever. We can't give away our whenua, our life. To stay strong we need land not bloody blue houses.'

'But they've got real flush toilets and polished floors,' argued Mum.

'Freeze your toes off in winter.'

'And some new furniture would be nice.'

'Who's going to pay for it? It's going to be tough enough paying the rent to those greedy beggars.' Dad always said politicians were slimier than eels in mud.

'But the rent counts as payments. We'll own it in a few years,' Mum argued.

'Don't count on it. What's the bet that they change the rules?'

Mum didn't give in. 'Well I'd like a place with electricity. Make things a whole lot easier. George and Pat say their house is pretty good, a bit small maybe.'

'Yeah! Where do the whanau sleep? They've built Pakeha houses – no room for whanau to come and stay – and it's windy as hell up there. Down here it's sheltered and close to the kaimoana. Why do you think we built the village here in the first place?

When Mum and Dad argued, Rewiti and I would slink away into the shadows. It didn't happen often. Like most of our people, Mum and Dad were good together – except when there was a party. At first everyone would be laughing, singing and playing the guitars. But as my eyelids drooped and the empty bottles piled up, the fights would start. Sometimes the police came and once Dad got taken to Auckland Hospital for a night because he 'fell into a tree', so Mum said. But I knew better when I saw Uncle Wiri's bandaged hand. He couldn't hold a beer bottle for ages. Lately, though, they were arguing without the parties.

I didn't care where we lived so long as Mum and Dad were happy. But that day, when I saw Koro cry, I realised this wasn't about moving houses. That fire was destroying more than our homes; it was destroying part of who we were. I saw it on Koro's face – as though his soul was leaking out of him with each silent tear. He hugged me close and I smelt his strength, his mana. Then he started singing a chant. It started quietly and gathered strength, ringing out above the crackling roar of the fire. Through the smoke I saw other figures slow their panicked running and shouting. They came towards him, as if the chant called them to calm down, draw together, stand firm, stand strong.

That first night on Boot Hill I lay in a new bed on crisp new sheets. Mum had spent up large without even paying a thing. She called it credit. Dad called it a 'bloody thorny rose'. Just a few weeks earlier, Dad and I had been sitting on the veranda of our old house.

'See those roses? Smell them,' he said.

I jumped off the veranda and into the garden. I sniffed every rose that grew along the front. I liked the dark red one best. Dad stepped down beside me.

'Beautiful isn't it?' he said. Before I could answer he brushed his hand against the rose bush. Blood, as deep red as the petals, slowly dripped from his finger.

I gasped. 'Dad, what did you do that for?'

He held his finger up, big drops of blood pooling in the dirt. 'Roses look and smell good but they have hidden thorns that hurt. Just like credit. It sounds good but it can rip you apart. Never buy anything on credit, Mere.' I didn't really understand but I remembered the blood.

3

I was just drifting off to sleep when Rewiti rushed into the bedroom. 'Wake up, sis.' He shook my shoulder. 'Something's happening down the hill. There's heaps of smoke. I think it's the marae!'

The government men had spared the marae and the graveyard. We might have to live up the hill but at least we could still bury our dead down at the urupa and gather together to welcome our visitors at the marae by the beach.

'See!' Rewiti was leaning out the window, straining to see more. The distant shouts of men drifted up the hill, along with the now familiar smell of smoke.

'Shut the window,' I coughed. 'I can't breathe. It stinks in here. All that smoke. Pooh! Did you do another fart?' I pulled the crispy new sheets over my head and curled up, trying to go back to sleep.

'Aw, shut up.' Rewiti leaned further out the window. 'Yes. It's the marae! I'm sure. How would that catch fire? It's miles away from the other buildings. I bet someone's done it. But who? Who'd burn down our marae?'

Boy, Rewiti could talk! Mostly I listened to what he said; he was brainy. Mum said he could be anything he wanted with those brains, maybe even a doctor. Rewiti said he was going to be the best fisherman in the tribe and have a boat. But tonight I wasn't listening to Rewiti raving on. I was exhausted and trying not to think about Teddy burning in the fire. I scrunched up even further under the blankets, hugging my pillow. Rewiti was right. Someone had burned down our marae. Most thought it was the government men, sneaking back to finish the job. Some weren't so sure. We never found out.

2

HELENE

Dr Helene Collins dug her fingers into the glass lolly jar, searching out the white jelly beans. Sure, they were meant for the children – a sweet distraction from any painful or frightening procedures – but that familiar woozy, inner shaking convinced her that one sweet coffee was not enough to get a girl through the day. She plonked the jar back on the rich mahogany desk and walked over to the full length windows. Pushing her hands into her lower back the way her Pilates instructor had taught her, she stared down at the Brisbane River. From her high-rise office window she watched the city cat skimming gracefully across the water as it ferried tired workers home for dinner. The buildings sprawled their shadows, smothering the last sparkles of sunlight. Man-made lights sprang to life all across the city.

Revived by the sugar she fished out three more of the little, white pick-me-ups and resolutely shut the lid. One last patient to write up: *Tom Peterson. Fever 39C°. Headache. No appetite. Senior partner – Buddle and Brown Legal.* Tucked in amongst the usual cholesterol and diabetes checks – and the portly gentleman who had strained his back dragging a full filing cabinet across his office – this was one of the first flu cases for the year. She continued her notes on Mr Peterson. *Lives alone. Recently separated.* The truth was his wife had kicked him out. Wouldn't any woman who caught her husband sleeping with his secretary? How many of these middle-aged businessmen traded in their first wife for a younger model? James would never do that, and yet …

Helene sighed. She loved her work, but her marriage was another story.

'Goodnight, Helene.' Melanie, the receptionist, leaned against the doorway, stuffing her high heels into her cavernous handbag and lacing up her running shoes.

'Watch out for spiders!' she laughed.

'Mel, did you really tell that patient he only had a few hours to live!' Mel's wild sense of humour sometimes pushed the boundaries but she had a heart of gold and reception had never been better managed.

Mel tossed her head and grinned. 'He knew I was joking. It put a smile back on his handsome face.'

Helene pressed 'Save' on Mr Peterson's notes and shut down her computer, recalling the strapping electrician with the redback spider bite. The tell-tale sweating red patch had been isolated with no evidence of systemic reaction. All he had needed was an ice-pack and panadol.

Melanie continued. 'Speaking of smiling, enjoy that Vietnamese restaurant. It's meant to be the best in town.'

Helene hurriedly gathered her things. Snapping her Oroton briefcase shut, she flung the matching handbag over her shoulder and headed for the car park. Dinner was booked for 7.30pm and it was already six. Hopefully James had bought the wine. As she sped up the Coronation Drive on-ramp she could see the rush hour traffic crawling along the edge of the river. She flicked her indicator and darted into the neighbouring lane – it seemed to be moving faster – then stamped on her brakes as a cascade of red brake lights flashed in front of her. Her slender fingers drummed an impatient beat on the steering wheel. Just at that moment the lights turned green and the cars sped off.

'Someone must be looking after me.' Helene caught herself uttering her mother's favourite saying. Not that her mother ever mentioned who she thought that 'someone' might be.

Helene swung into her driveway, the car wheels crunching on the white pebbles. She grabbed her bag and raced up the paved front path. The front door was ajar. Coloured light danced on the rich polished floor boards of the front hallway, the stained glass window above the door illuminated by a street light.

'Hi, darling.' James wandered out of the bedroom wearing only jeans and rubbing his still wet hair with a towel. He reached out to hug her. 'How was your day?'

'Busy.' She gave him a half-hug and brushed past him into the bedroom, kicking off her red wedge heels and dumping her bag on the bed. 'Russell said to say 'hi'. You didn't tell me you saw him.'

'It was just a wave across the car park. He was busy with a group of mates.' James followed her into their bathroom and leant against the white tiled wall. His gaze roamed over her naked body as she let the cool shower refresh her.

'Mates?' she laughed. 'They were most likely clients. If he's not "entertaining" them in his corporate box, it's on the golf course. I've never met anyone who lives and breathes his business like Russell.'

James passed her a fluffy white towel, letting his hands linger on her body. Helene quickly wrapped the towel around her. No time for that now. Dinner was only an hour away. He got the message.

'Mum phoned today. She wondered if a friend of hers could stay in the guest house for a few weeks. She's writing a book or a memoir or something, and needs somewhere quiet for a few weeks. Mum said she could stay with them on the farm but they'd probably chat too much. It's been years since they've seen each other.'

'Sounds fine. It just sits there empty most of the time except when your parents come down to visit. We probably won't even notice she's there.' Helene studied her wardrobe. Should she wear the short black cocktail dress or her black Italian pants? Nicolette would be looking stunning as usual. Blonde, tanned and slim, she was the perfect coat hanger. Nicolette collected men like Helene collected shoes: expensive and gorgeous but easily discarded when another caught her eye. She wriggled into the black cocktail dress and smoothed it out over her hips. It wouldn't hurt to look good for whoever Nicolette brought along. On the way out she sprayed a haze of Chanel in front of her and stepped through the suspended scent. James locked the door and followed her out to the car. 'You look nice.'

'Thanks.' Did he really mean it or was it part of the married routine? The words fell short of her heart.

James backed the car out of the driveway. 'She's Maori, you know.'

'Who's Maori?'

'Mum's friend. Her name is Mere – like Mary but it sounds different when she says it. She sort of rolls the r. It's the Maori version of Mary.'

'Can your mum speak Maori?'

'Not fluently but she knows a little from her childhood. She and Mere were best friends as kids in New Zealand until Mum's family moved here.'

Helene checked her make-up in the mirror. 'When did you say she was coming?'

'This weekend, if that's okay. We just need to replace a couple of light bulbs and check the oven is working. Apparently she's a great cook, just like Mum.'

'I'm not sure if I'm into that doting stay-at-home mother thing. It didn't work too well for my mum.'

James patted her on the knee. 'Don't worry. You'll probably change your mind when we have our own kids.'

Helene glanced out the window and tried not to grimace.

They pulled into a parking space opposite the restaurant just as Nicolette swung her long, tanned legs out of her red convertible. She tugged down her skimpy gold skirt and waved a French manicured hand at the man strolling down the street towards her.

'I think that's Brad Smith. He's one of the Reds top players.' James locked the car.

'Probably,' replied Helene. 'Nicolette has been raving about him since they met at the sports awards last month.'

'What about that radio announcer she was going out with?'

'She dumped him at the same party.'

They crossed the road to Nicolette who by now had her arms stretched up and wrapped around the man's neck, whispering something in his ear. Helene noticed how his hands kept slipping from her waist to her hips. He couldn't get enough of her.

'Hi, guys.' Nicolette untangled herself from Brad as they approached. 'How are you?'

The emphasis was on the 'are' and as usual, Helene thought, it was rhetorical. She had more to say.

'This is Brad. He's in the Reds. Although, James, you probably already know that.'

She batted her mascara-laden lashes at James and then returned her attention to Brad.

'Helene's not so into rugby but she may have seen you on television. Have you, Helene?'

'I think I did see you a few weeks ago on the news.' Helene smiled at Brad. Of course she had seen him on television, but not playing rugby. His name constantly appeared in the press linked with various models, television presenters and the occasional nightclub brawl.

'Good to meet you.' James shook Brad's hand. 'You were great in the game last weekend.'

'Thanks, mate. It was a tough one.' Brad grinned.

As the men discussed details of last week's match, Nicolette led the way into the tiny, packed restaurant. Helene wondered how they would hear each other over the din of so many enthusiastic diners but the atmosphere certainly made up for it. A waiter seated them in a corner by the window and as they perused the menu Nicolette snuggled into Brad.

'Choose the rice paper rolls. They're the best.'

'Really?' James asked. 'So you've been here before?'

'Plenty of times. It's my absolute favourite for entertaining clients.'

'I'm not really into chilli,' said Brad frowning at the menu as though it was written in Vietnamese.

'Don't worry, darling. We'll make sure we order something with plenty of meat and no chilli just for you. We need to keep your strength up for the game this weekend. And tonight!'

Brad masked his ravenous grin with a swig of beer.

The waiter soon brought out a platter of enormous Vietnamese spring rolls, the moist rice paper wrapped around whole prawns, minced pork, grated carrot, coriander and fragrant mint. Helene spooned the accompanying sauce over her roll and took a bite. Rugby talk swirled around her. The men discussed which team was likely to win the Super 15, which players had accepted overseas contracts for next season and when the Reds star goal kicker might be back on the field after his knee construction. Helene tried to add in the odd comment – things she had heard on the radio or at work – but her attention kept shifting to the neighbouring diners. From the corner of her eye she noticed furtive, admiring glances in their direction from a table of giggling young women. There must have been at least four bottles of wine and as many glasses of beer on the table. Helene watched one of the girls fluff out her auburn hair with her fingers, push her chair backwards with her tiny denim cling-wrapped bottom and teeter over to Brad. Gripping the back of his chair with one ring-laden hand, she tapped him on the shoulder with an impossibly long red finger-nail.

'Hi, Brad. Would you mind if my friends took a photo of us?'

Brad turned sideways in his chair, smiled at the table of star-struck girls and nodded. 'Sure.'

The redhead draped herself across his lap, leaned into his shoulder and wound one arm around his neck. Brad's glance dropped briefly to the girl's ample cleavage bursting above a green scoop neck top. Then he flashed a practised smile at the camera.

'Thanks so much.' The girl leaned provocatively towards him, kissed him on the cheek, winked at James and sauntered back to her envious friends.

After the main course had been cleared and they were waiting for coffee Nicolette drew Helene aside and whispered behind her wine glass, 'So what do you think?'

'Gorgeous and obviously in demand,' Helene whispered back with a subtle nod towards the by now raucous table of girls who continued to ogle Brad and occasionally James.

Nicolette winked. 'I know. Hey, let's catch up for coffee next week and we can have a chat.'

'I can't wait.' Chatting with Nicolette was better than any television soap opera.

Helene snuggled into her pashmina on the way home, deep in thought. Balmy summer nights had given way to the crisp, cool evenings of autumn where the heat of the day evaporated rapidly into the clear sky. James was humming to the radio as he drove, seemingly content.

'Brad's pretty cool, isn't he? He said he could get us good seats to next weekend's game. Do you want to go? It's heaps better in real life than on television.'

'I'll probably have to work next weekend.'

Her excuse sounded lame and she knew it, but didn't care. She was too caught up with the thoughts flying around her head. *The spark's gone out of our marriage. Look at Brad and Nicolette. When was the last time James treated me like that?* Their fifth wedding anniversary was coming up in a few months. Would James arrange some romantic surprise? Of course not. They were in a dull routine. Each night James plonked in front of the television, riveted to the news and rugby. Her efforts to make meaningful conversation were about as effective as a watering can in the outback. If it didn't involve work or sport he wasn't interested, unlike Nicolette and Brad who certainly wouldn't be watching sport tonight.

'Are you okay?' James parked the car and gave her that searching 'What's up?' look.

'Fine.'

Helene tried to sound happy but it came out as forced politeness, the tone reserved for acquaintances or strangers. She saw his eyes dim and felt the distance between them grow a little more.

'I'm just tired.'

'Me too,' James replied.

Helene was already curled up on her side of the bed when James jumped in and tried to kiss her. She kept her eyes closed, feigning sleep.

3

The river flows wide and smooth as she drifts on the current, guiding the raft downstream with an occasional dip of the paddle. Coloured flowers and lush green growth spill down the riverbank. Warm sunlight bathes her body. She dips her paddle in again and sighs.

She hears it before she sees it – a roaring wall of water rushing towards her, intent on destruction. It smashes into the raft, hurtling it forwards. Furious white water batters and spins the raft. Ominous boulders loom before her. Clutching the paddle she frantically stabs the water forwards, then backwards. She flings herself to one side of the raft, then to the other, weaving it through the deadly obstacle course. Fear and excitement clench her muscles. Exhilaration sears her mind. She can do this. She is still in control.

The river narrows and drops. Steep banks of loose gravel rise on both sides. Even as she battles the rapids she senses two people observing her – a man and a woman – standing halfway up the steep bank. The man is in his thirties and the woman in her sixties. They exude peace and tranquillity, yet somehow great power. Although she is hurtling through the rapids, they are always in view, right there, halfway up the riverbank. The man touches the woman on the shoulder as if giving a signal. The woman smiles and reaches out her hand. She knows she can grasp this woman's hand and be pulled to safety. But the rapids are becoming wilder. She needs both hands on the paddle. The river swerves sharply to the left. The raft smashes into a rock. Her paddle snaps. Just ahead, the river disappears. The raft is out of control. She grasps the sides and screams as it plummets over the waterfall ...

Helene woke with a start. There it was again – that dream about the raft. She wiped the perspiration from her forehead and forced herself to take deep breaths to slow her racing heart. What would have happened if she'd gone over the waterfall? Who were the man and woman on the hillside? She didn't usually take too much notice of dreams, but this one was so vivid and terrifying. Wide awake, she jumped out of bed, trying to pull herself back to the real world, but the dream remained, planted just at the edge of her subconscious.

4

JAMES

James looked at himself in the mirror, his face half covered with shaving foam as he finished getting ready for work. Today was a big day. He had to look sharp. If Bob Campbell became a client, with his multi-million dollar travel firm, it would be just the coup he needed to consolidate his fledgling business. He splashed his face with cold water. His cheeks still glowed from his early morning run and his hair glistened wet from the shower. Hopefully he hadn't woken Helene. She had been distant lately, especially in the bedroom, which wasn't good. Maybe some extra sleep would restore her energy. He hoped so. A good night peck on the cheek wasn't enough to relieve the day's tension nor did it reassure him that Helene thought this new business was a good idea.

He was already sitting at the recycled teak dining table, sorting through a pile of papers when Helene padded into the kitchen, still in her silk pyjamas.

'I didn't hear you get up this morning.' She stifled an early morning yawn. 'It must have been early. Have you got a busy day?'

James stopped his paper shuffling for a moment and took a gulp of his black coffee. 'There's a report somewhere here that I need for my meeting this morning. I need to be on the ball for this guy. You know, Helene, if I win this contract it will double our income.'

Helene pulled a glass from the cupboard and filled it with water. 'That would be good. It might cover your expensive rent at last.'

Her barbed retort struck deep.

'Don't you think I'm concerned about the rent too? It doesn't help to keep going on about it. At least you could try to support me.'

'I don't keep going on about it. I hardly ever mention it.'

'Yes you do. I can tell you don't think I can do this. You're always so negative.' He riffled through the papers, finally finding the report he needed.

'I'm just worried about the money. That you've over-committed yourself.'

'If I get this client today, the money won't be a problem. How do you expect me to succeed without taking some risks?'

He threw his papers into his bag and tipped the half-drunk coffee down the sink. 'I've got to go.' She seemed about to say something else but he didn't have time for arguments. He was already late. *I'll get this contract and then she'll be happy.* He hurried down the hall and out the front door. A gust of wind caught it and slammed it shut.

5

HELENE

Helene arrived at work to find Mel, foot up on the desk, painting her toenails.

'What a great sight for the patients.'

Mel whipped her foot off the desk and grinned. 'Helene! I didn't expect you in so early. I usually have a good ten minutes before any of you doctors arrive.'

'James had an early meeting so I thought I may as well come in and catch up on my paper work.

She made herself an extra strong coffee and carried it back to her office, pushing the door shut with her foot. Dumping her handbag on the floor, she took a much needed sip of the sweet brew and stared out the window, seeing nothing. All she could think about was their argument this morning and the sudden sinking in the pit of her stomach as James had stormed out and slammed the door. The sensation was similar to flying with her grandad as he lurched the plane up and down, but that was exhilarating; this was just draining.

Warm sunlight bathed the office but it wasn't enough to thaw the ice fragment embedding deeper into her heart.

Ever since his move into the city James had become obsessed with work. When had they last had fun or laughed together? When had they last had a holiday? How could they afford one? The bank seemed to gobble every spare cent. Was he really capable of pulling off his ambitious plan? She wasn't sure.

A light tap at the door broke Helene's reverie. Mel dumped a pile of papers on the desk and perched next to them.

'Would you have time to sign these off this morning? Then I can post them out today.'

Helene fixed on her professional mask. Her personal problems could take a back seat. It was a relief to be able to shut them out and focus on work. 'Sure. I'll do them in a minute. So how's today shaping up?'

'Quieter than yesterday. But there is a new drug rep coming to see you which should be exciting.'

'A drug rep? Exciting?'

'Just wait until you see him, Helene. I know you don't like reps but I'm sure you will want to see this one! He's totally, drop dead gorgeous. I don't care what he's selling; he can talk to me any time!'

'Well I do need to take a bit of interest in his product too. Do you know what it is?'

'No idea! But he's from MSD. Anyway, I've scheduled ten minutes for you to see him at eleven this morning.'

Helene signed the reports, cringing at the needless radiology referrals, all to satisfy a couple of obsessive patients that had self-diagnosed their condition on the internet. She gathered up the papers and headed down the corridor towards reception. As she passed the nurse's room she heard a hacking cough. Judith was bracing herself against the narrow patient's bed, her body doubled over.

'Judith, are you all right? Here, sit down.' Helene helped her to a chair and felt her forehead. She had a fever, another early case of the flu.

'You can't work like this. You need to go home and rest. Let me call you a taxi.'

Judith smiled through watery eyes. 'You're right,' she wheezed. 'I thought I'd be okay once I got to work. But don't call a cab. The kids are all at school so Mike can come and get me. I suppose that's one good thing about redundancy.' Her sigh set off another coughing spasm. Helene rubbed her back with a gentle circular motion, soothing away the violent convulsions.

'I am so sorry about Mike losing his job. It must be very stressful,' she said.

'I haven't told anyone here yet but that's not the worst of it. We've had to sell the house for less than what we paid for it. The packers come next week.' She looked completely drained.

'That's terrible. Do you have somewhere to go?'

'We're staying with Mike's brother for a while.' She looked up at Helene, her nose and cheeks a congested red in her blanched face.

'I know I should be grateful. I am grateful. But not having your own home, living off the charity of someone else, you have no idea how pathetic it makes me feel.'

Helene grasped her hand. 'Judith, you are not pathetic, you're a highly competent nurse and we couldn't do without you here. Now go home and rest. And please let me know if I can do anything to help.' It sounded so lame, like throwing an inflatable life vest at the Titanic. She had heard the same words so many times before and cringed even as she spoke them.

Judith sat up a little straighter. 'I'm sure we will be fine. Just telling someone has helped me feel a bit better. I really do appreciate it.'

Helene gave her a big hug. Judith may think no one knew how she felt but she had a very good idea indeed.

***

Mel was right: the morning list was quieter than usual which gave Helene plenty of time to write up patient notes and check out a new medical referral website. She did neither. Judith's situation had ripped open memories like pulling a plaster off an unhealed wound. The harder she tried to not remember that terrible time, the more the memories flooded in until she could think of nothing else.

On the day her life changed forever she had been practising dive bombs in the pool. She had just done a particularly good one. Her tightly curled body hit the water at the perfect angle and dropped straight to the bottom. She unfurled her gangly, almost teenage legs and erupted from the pool, eager to see if the splash had hit its target. A deluged patch of terracotta pavers glistened orange as the water hurried back to the pool, trying to evade evaporation. She squinted through rivulets of water at the dark, patent leather leaves of the agapanthus bobbing their mauve and white heads in approval. Droplets of water shimmered like fairy bubbles on the glossy green leaves. She had hit her target.

'Helene, me darling.' She spun around at the sound of her dad's rich Irish lilt.

'Daddy! Did you see that dive bomb? I hit the agapanthus but I bet I could get even further. Watch me!' She clambered out of the pool ready to impress him with her best ever bomb. It didn't occur to her until later why he was home in the afternoon. He never came home in the daylight. He glanced at his watch and wiped the back of his hand across his brow. Why was he wearing those fancy clothes around the pool anyway? It was far too hot.

'It was amazing, my love.' He shielded his face with his hand and looked up at the gum tree rustling above them. 'Do you know I'm sure I can see a koala up there wiping a drop from his nose?'

'Daddy, don't be silly. There's no koala up there.'

'Of course there is. Can't you see him tucked up on that branch? He looks a might grumpy, don't you think?'

She shielded her eyes and peered upwards, willing herself to see the koala.

'Now I see him. He's licking water off the gum leaves.'

Daddy laughed. It was his shoe lace laugh: all tied up in knots it hardly managed to squeeze out at all. She liked her Daddy's man-laugh the best. It was a raucous, rolling laugh that swept you up and carried you to exciting, never seen before places. It reminded her of Daddy dancing Mum around the kitchen, or crawling through her cushion cave to find buried treasure.

'Come here, my angel.' He didn't look right. It was as though he was about to dive in a freezing cold pool. She scampered across the steaming pavers, dripping like a melting pineapple ice-block in her new yellow swimsuit. He stepped sideways to avoid the water which was pooling in the paving cracks and heading for his shiny black shoes.

'I have to go away for a while.'

'For your work?'

'Yes, for my work. It's a new job with lots of money.'

'Will you be back to see me in the school concert? You promised you would come this year. I'm an angel and I even get to speak.' He stepped backwards avoiding the water that persisted in tracking his shoes.

'I'll try, me sweetheart.'

That was as good as yes to her. He would be there this time. She threw her damp arms around his waist and hugged him. 'And Daddy, when you come back will you do dive bombs with me?'

He gently extricated himself from her grasp and brushed the water from his suit. 'Careful, I can't be looking like a drowned rat on me first day now, can I?' He bent down and kissed her on the forehead. 'Now you be good for your Mammy and look after her.'

He left before she could reply, striding away without a backwards glance. She ran after him ready to give him one more hug but then she saw her Mum. She looked like a papier mâché doll, her face all blotchy and scrambled. She was swaying against the kitchen wall with her arms hugged tightly around her as though she had a bad stomach ache.

She heard the toot of a car and raced around the side of the house in time to see Daddy lug two big suitcases into the taxi and slam the boot. He pulled a silver flask from his suit jacket and took a swig before jumping into the cab and slamming the door. The cab pulled away. She waved. Daddy never looked back.

The next day a man came and told them the bank now owned the house. They had three days to move out. Daddy never came back. There was no job. No money. No koala.

6

Eleven o'clock soon arrived and Helene hurried out to the bathroom to splash the memories away and touch up her makeup. She returned just as Mel ushered the tall, blond rep into her office. Helene glanced at his biceps bulging beneath the rolled up sleeves of a pale blue business shirt as he held his briefcase in one hand and reached out the other to shake her hand.

'Good morning, Dr Collins. I'm Ben Erskine from MSD. It's good to meet you.' He looked straight into her eyes. He seemed confident, self-assured but not arrogant.

Helene relaxed and smiled.

'Good to meet you too. Please sit down.' She motioned to a small red couch and chair arranged around a glass coffee table near the windows. 'Would you like a coffee or tea, or a cold drink?'

He wore a leather band around his smooth, tanned wrist and must have taken out his earring for the meeting. Perhaps he was a surfer.

'No thanks. I know you're busy so I'll get straight to the point.' He pulled some brochures and a pack of tablets out from his bag. 'This is our latest cholesterol lowering medication. It's just passed TGA approval and it has some significant advantages over the current medications available, particularly for your hypertensive patients.'

Helene tried hard to concentrate on the technical details and research he presented but her mind kept drifting. He was certainly good looking, Mel had been right about that.

The meeting finished. Helene patted the pile of prescription pads and brochures.

21

'Very interesting. I'll read through these and discuss it with my colleagues. There are a couple of patients who might benefit from this medication. I'll let you know.'

Ben stood up and shook Helene's hand. He held it a little longer than usual and his green eyes lingered. Helene felt her heart beat a little more rapidly. 'Thanks for your time, Dr Collins. I hope that next time we meet we'll have time for that drink. Please call me if you have any questions.'

Helene shut the office door and leant against it, taking a deep breath to steady herself. She was acting like a besotted teenager over a complete stranger who showed her a little attention. Was she that desperate?

The phone rang. Helene crossed the room and picked it up. 'Dr Collins speaking.'

'Hi, it's me. My meeting went really well.' James' words tumbled out in excitement. 'He wants to sign me up as his exclusive agency. I can hardly believe it. Isn't it great?'

Helene fumbled around trying to replace swirling thoughts of leather wristbands with James' meeting. Reality finally kicked in – the new client.

'Oh, yes, that's wonderful. You sound very excited.'

'I am. This is fantastic! Let's celebrate tonight. What's for dinner?'

The simple question inflamed angry embers of resentment. What was she? His slave?

'I have no idea,' she retorted. 'I haven't had time to think about dinner. I've been working, remember? And I'm really busy. That's good about your meeting but I've got to go. Bye.'

She tried not to slam down the phone. What's for dinner indeed! His mother might enjoy reciting what delectable morsels she planned to prepare for her mighty working husband but she was different. She had her own career – and it wasn't cooking.

It was only a short walk to the Botanical Gardens – a tranquil park separating the city from the river. She watched as a horse-drawn carriage drew up to the wrought iron gates at the gardens' entrance. It was a popular place for weddings, even on a Friday. The groom jumped down, and like a knight in shining armour, helped his bride step out onto the grass. Bridesmaids dressed in pink hurried towards her from their BMW. It was the idyllic bridal scene.

Then the groom abandoned his bride, grabbed a few cans of cold beer from an eski and tossed them to his groomsmen. They stood in a huddle drinking, joking and watching the harried wedding photographer set up his cameras. And where was the gentle, tentative bride? That image also vanished as the bride dragged on a cigarette, then passed it to her bridesmaid, taking great care not to spill ash on her white dress.

What a reflection of life, Helene mused. People worked so hard to make it appear perfect but the image lasted only an instant before real people with all their flaws stepped in and wrecked it. *Just like me and James. He takes me for granted.*

The laboured hiss of a truck's air brakes jerked Helene back to the present. She glanced at her watch, swigged her water bottle and hurried back to work. The afternoon passed in a flurry of patients: sick and not so sick, happy and unhappy, relaxed and hassled, with too many children or not enough. Before she knew it, Helene was tidying her desk and packing her briefcase.

'Hey, Helene. Have a great weekend,' called Russell through the open door of his office.

'Are you and James doing anything exciting?'

'Probably not. What about you?'

'My usual round of golf and taking a few clients to the rugby tomorrow night. Should be a fantastic game. You and James must come along one night.'

'That would be great. James would love it.' Helene forced herself to sound enthusiastic. What was it about rugby that got men so excited?

'Oh, I almost forgot. Ben from MSD sent me details of the conference they are sponsoring in Noosa. I thought you might like to go - on the company of course.'

She suddenly felt brighter. A weekend at Noosa was exactly what she needed. 'I'd love to.'

7

JAMES

James sprawled out on the leather lounge, stubby in one hand, remote control in the other. The rugby was about to start and he felt great. This was the break he'd been hoping for. The deal they had discussed today was even better than he had hoped. Finally he had a foot in the door of the tightly competitive industry. And when he told Helene how much they were paying she would be amazed.

The front door clicked open and shut. He jumped out of his seat to greet her.

'Hi, darling.' He threw his arms around her and smacked her on the lips. 'Isn't it great? I bought us some wine. We can have it in front of the game.'

Helene glanced past him at the television, her smile fading. 'Oh, okay.'

James stepped back. 'I thought you would be a bit more enthusiastic than that. This is an amazing deal.'

'I am pleased. I'm just tired.' She dropped her bag on the side table and headed for the kitchen. James returned to his seat and picked up his stubby. The players were warming up on the field. He called out to Helene. 'I bought you some bread. How about we have toasted sandwiches?'

Helene reappeared, looking surprisingly grumpy. 'So you're just going to sit in front of the television while I cook dinner?'

'Well if you are not hungry, I can wait. Bring the wine and come and watch the game with me.' He patted the seat next to him.

She didn't move. 'Why do you assume that I should cook just because I am the woman? I'm not your mother.'

James gripped his beer bottle a little harder. 'What's wrong with my mother?'

'Nothing's wrong with your mother. It's just that I'm not like her.'

'I thought you liked cooking.'

'I do but not when you expect me to do it every night. I have a job too, you know.'

'Well with this new contract you don't have to work. I could support us both.'

Helene planted her hands on her hips. 'I don't need to be supported. I can take care of myself. I always have.'

James glanced at the television. The ref had just blown the whistle to start the game and he was missing it because of some stupid argument. 'Look Helene, I bought that wine for us to celebrate…'

'In front of the rugby?

'Why not?'

'Because it's boring, we don't talk and I don't want to celebrate some contract that makes you think I can just quit my job. My work is important. I save people's lives; you only save pictures.'

Her words hit him like a rugby fullback. Heat rushed to his face. 'Nothing I do is ever good enough for you. If you don't want to watch the game, fine, I'll go and watch it somewhere else.' He jumped out of his seat and grabbed his keys from the side table.

Helene reached out to touch him. 'Stop over-reacting. I was only telling you how I feel.'

He shook her hand off. 'I just want a few quiet beers in peace. I'm going to John's.' He marched out the door.

He was already regretting his anger as he headed to the car. It was her comment about him only saving pictures that had done it. This computer graphics business was his dream, his baby. He had originally set up in a cheap, outer suburb with his mate, John. But after a few years of building the business together John had succumbed to the lure of a multi-national company offering a safe contract and big money. That hadn't deterred him. He revised his business plan and transformed what might have been a deathblow into a potentially lucrative venture. But it came with risk: the refurbished cottage in Milton was ideal as an office but the rent was twice what he'd paid in the suburbs.

What would his parents think if they knew how much he had borrowed? His dad wasn't one for debt unless it was for something 'worthwhile' like land. It was fine to leave the farm and go to university so long as he eventually returned. His two older brothers were managing farms and the home farm sat there waiting to receive him into his pre-appointed slot. When he'd announced his plans to stay in the city and set up a computer company his mother had tried to be supportive but he could tell she was disappointed. She still dropped hints every time he and Helene visited.

'The local doctor is retiring soon. They'll be looking for someone to replace him. This is such a wonderful place to bring up children. No crime or pollution.'

His dad was more direct. His dismissive comments and friendly jibes shredded his confidence.

'Drawing pictures on computers, that's not real work. You city slickers don't know the meaning of hard work, with your soft hands and air-conditioned offices.' He wished his dad would take him seriously.

It was different with Helene. They were meant to be a team. Wasn't she meant to support him? He could handle his parents' doubts but not Helene's. If she didn't think he was any good, he may as well quit now. What was the point? He fired up the ignition and headed to John's.

8

HELENE

James wasn't home when Helene woke early Saturday morning. Perhaps he had crept in late and gone out this morning for a run or to the bakery? She checked the spare bedroom for signs of disturbance. The sight of the untouched bed made her sigh and rub away the tearful tingling behind her eyes. This wasn't how their life was meant to be. This wasn't how she had planned it. The phone rang in her bedroom. She wandered back and sat cross-legged on the crumpled sheets to answer it.

'Helene. Hi. It's me, Jacqueline. I hope I didn't wake you and James. Sorry. I'm desperate. Do you have any baking powder? I said I would take fairy cakes to the birthday party this morning – one of the twins little friends – and I can't wait for the shops to open. We have to leave here at nine.'

'How did you ever manage your job in Sydney?'

'I wasn't sleep deprived with three kids coming in and out of our bed half the night. That doesn't do a whole lot for your presence of mind! Enjoy your sleep-ins while you can, that's all I can say.'

Jacqueline, her older sister, was a bundle of energy with a mind to match. She seemed to relish the whole motherhood thing even though it seemed such a waste to have thrown away her career.

'Merchant banking and motherhood don't mix. One had to go,' Jacqueline had explained to Helene when she first arrived in Brisbane, heavily pregnant and newly jobless. 'Chris's firm have opened a branch here in Brisbane so it's worked out perfectly. He can run that while I have babies. I'm sure I'll get back to work sometime.'

27

Five years and three kids later, her suits still hung in mothballs and the only meetings she attended were play-dates and birthday parties.

Helene smiled. Her mad, energetic sister was a breath of fresh air.

'Sure. I've got some baking powder and I need a run. I'll jog around in a minute.'

'You're a god-send, Helene. Oops. Got to go – we've just had an accident on the carpet. I'll be so glad when toilet training is over!'

Helene pulled on her running shorts and a tank top. She tied her straight hair up in a ponytail, flipped it through a white cap and went to the kitchen to get the baking powder. No sign of James. He had never stayed out all night before. What a way to start the weekend. She needed a good long run to drain off all this emotion.

By the time she reached the top of the first hill her heart was racing and her legs burning. The pain was perversely invigorating. She gulped in the crisp morning air and relaxed into a gentle jog along still sleepy streets. Hardly any cars to wonder why she was out jogging with a packet of baking powder!

***

Helene was stretching and cooling down after her run when a taxi pulled up. A Maori woman dressed in loose black trousers and sturdy shoes climbed out. Her smiling face shimmered with perspiration and a tiny rivulet of sweat trickled past the green stone pendant that hung around her neck. It must be James' mum's friend. Helene hurried down the steps to greet her.

'Hi. You must be Mere. Welcome to Brisbane.'

Mere put her hand up to her mouth and coughed, then held out her other hand in greeting. 'And you must be Helene. Thank you for allowing me to stay, especially at such short notice. It's very kind of you.' She wiped her forehead and fanned herself with her hand. 'Whew, it's hot!'

'I guess it's a bit warmer than New Zealand. How was your flight?'

'Wonderful. I sat next to a family of six children, all chatting, giggling and not too much arguing. They keep you young.'

'My sister has three but I'm not sure whether she feels so young.' Jacqueline had looked just the opposite this morning as she raced from the kitchen to the laundry to the bathroom, mixing muffins, throwing dirty clothes in the wash and scraping food scraps off the floor while trying to slap on some lipstick and mascara.

'It's busy but they're such a blessing. I have five children, nineteen grandchildren and three great-grandchildren.'

'No wonder you needed to get away!' She didn't look much older than her own parents yet she had so many children. She was clearly one of those women who had made a career out of being a mother. She picked up Mere's bag. 'I'll show you where you are staying.'

They walked down the driveway to the tiny white-washed building with blue shutters and a rose pink door. Mere followed Helene into the bright, modern lounge. 'It's lovely!'

Helene flung open the windows. 'I've put some milk in the fridge and a few groceries in the cupboard. The shops are only a ten minute walk down the road.'

Mere dumped a heavy-looking briefcase on a chair. 'Now tell me about you and James. Shirley said you didn't have children but were both very busy with your jobs. You're a doctor, aren't you?'

'Yes, in the city.'

'And James? Shirley said that he's just set up his own graphic design business. He sounds a talented young man. I've never been able to get past e-mails and word processing myself.'

'I guess he is.' She tried not to feel put out that Mere seemed more impressed with James' work than hers. Guilt squirmed inside as she recalled their argument the night before.

'Well, dearie, I know it's only breakfast time for you but I've been up since three Australian time and I'm ready for a cup of tea. Would you like one?' She filled the kettle with water and switched it on.

'Just a quick one, thanks Mere. I have a hair appointment at eleven.'

Helene pulled out cups and tea bags while Mere put milk and sugar on the tiny wooden dining table.

'So where is James this morning?' Mere poured milk into her tea followed by two generous spoonfuls of sugar.

'Um, well, I think he's with his friend.'

'Oh?'

She shouldn't be telling Mere her personal problems. She didn't even know her, except through James' mum, which made it worse. But that single syllable question had such warm concern attached to it that she couldn't help herself.

'We had an argument last night and he walked out. He hasn't been home since.'

'I see.' Mere took a slow sip of her tea. 'And how are you feeling about it?'

Helene chewed her lip. 'I don't know. I just hate these arguments,' she sighed.

'Saying sorry only takes a moment.'

'I suppose so. But why should it be me to say sorry? He's the one that treats me like his mother – expecting me to do all the cooking and cleaning – and if I can fit in my job, that's just an optional extra. He even suggested I could give it up! No thanks. My job is the one thing that makes me feel good.'

Mere sat thoughtfully. 'So you feel he doesn't appreciate you.'

'Exactly.'

'And do you appreciate him?' The gentle question sliced through Helene's indignation.

'Of course I do,' she replied, surprised at her own defensiveness.

'Good. That's all that's needed. Too many of us don't appreciate what we've got until it's gone.' Her bright eyes dimmed, as though she was remembering something sad. It was only a moment but it made Helene wonder.

'James tells me you're writing a book?'

'It's more a memoir than a book. I want to record certain events in my life, lessons I've learned, for my grandchildren. In the old days, Maori passed their stories down orally but the only way I'd get my grandkids to sit still for more than a few minutes is if they were mesmerised by some computer game.'

'I know. I bribe the kids who come to see me with jelly beans. It works for a few minutes.' They laughed together and the conversation moved to food. She didn't notice the time until she glanced at her watch.

'My hair appointment. I'm running late. Just make yourself at home. Hopefully James will be back soon.'

Mere walked her to the door and as Helene turned to say goodbye she took hold of both her hands, looked her in the eyes and smiled. 'Everything will be fine with you and James.'

It was the statement of a fact, not a vain hope or platitude. How could Mere, who had only just met her, be so sure?

She grabbed her handbag and car keys from inside the house. Her hair desperately needed a trim and if anyone could take her mind off herself it was Raphael. Raphael and his partner, Antonio, ran a thriving salon in Paddington. Their splashy advertisements promoted them as 'Stylists to the Stars'. It was true. She'd seen plenty of celebrities, looking anything but their best, being pampered and flattered by the flamboyant duo. Arriving at the salon she squeezed into a car space on the street. As she pushed open the salon's sleek glass door Raphael greeted her from behind the counter, gushing in his usual flamboyant manner.

'Darling, you look gorgeous.' His massive gold rings glittered as he took her hand, kissed it and led her to sit in front of a gilt edged mirror. 'If I wasn't taken, you just wouldn't be safe here,' he teased in a theatrical whisper. Antonio, his partner, pursed his lips and snipped his client's hair a little more forcefully. Half the fun of coming here was seeing the constant tiffs between these two.

'Shall we do something a little different today?' Raphael ran his bird-fingers through her hair, lifting it up and letting it fall.

'Just a trim today, thanks Raphael.'

'Speaking of trims,' he lowered his voice, 'we had a bit of drama in here last week …'

9

JAMES

James filled a tall glass with water, gulped it down, then filled it again and wandered out to the back veranda. His head felt thick and his mouth dry. He and John had knocked back a fair few last night. He couldn't even remember when he'd crashed on the couch but he'd woken up cradling a half-drunk bottle of beer. The windows of the flat were open. Mere must have arrived. He walked across the back lawn and knocked on the door. No answer. He peered through the window. A laptop was set up on the dining table and a large book lay open beside it. Two cups sat on the kitchen bench.

'Hello.'

The voice behind him made him jump. He turned to see a stately Maori woman with a beaming smile walking up the driveway. It had to be Mere.

'I hope I didn't scare you.' She lowered two bulging grocery bags to the ground and stepped forward to shake his hand. 'I'm Mere and I can tell you're Shirley's boy. You've got the same green eyes.'

'It's a dead giveaway, I know,' laughed James. 'I could never get away with anything when I was a kid; they all knew who I was. It's good to meet you at last. Mum used to talk about you often as we grew up. You were best friends, weren't you?'

'Yes, we lived in the same street and went to the same school. There weren't too many Pakehas, I mean white people, where we lived but your mum and I became friends from the first day we started school. She even gave me her teddy bear. It was so special – the first present I'd ever received.'

'Do you still have it?'

'No, it was burned in a fire.'

'That's too bad. But I guess it's the memory that counts.'

Mere took off her straw hat, wiped her forehead and coughed. She looked up at James and smiled. 'Yes, we always have the memories. Now if I remember correctly you and Helene have been married for five years, is that right? She's a lovely, kind girl. I met her when I arrived and she got me settled in before she went to the hair salon.'

'How do you know how long we've been married? I can hardly remember myself.'

'Shirley keeps me up to date with what you and your brothers are doing and I have a pretty good memory for dates.'

'You must have.' James looked at the grocery bags. 'Let me help you with those. They look heavy.' He picked them up and carried them into the flat. Mere started unpacking potatoes, flour, sugar and oats.

'Just a few basics to get me started.' She turned to James. 'It's so kind of you to allow me to stay.'

'It's no problem. We'll give you a spare key to the house so you can use the laundry and if you need any extra food, just help yourself to the kitchen. Now, do you need anything else?'

'I'm perfectly fine, thank you, dear. But I am concerned that I've arrived at rather an awkward time. I don't want to add any stress to you and Helene.'

Helene must have told her about last night. 'It's just this new business. It's a challenge but I know it will work. Helene doesn't. Between her and my parents I have the best critics a man could want.' He laughed dismissively.

'Do your farm dogs ever have fleas?'

What on earth did fleas have to do with anything? He answered, curious. 'Yeah, sometimes they go crazy scratching.'

'Well a flea has one mission in life: to find a safe, warm place that will supply all its needs, like a dog's back. When we get married we're a bit like a flea that thinks it's found a dog's back. But we're wrong. The person we've married is actually another flea who thinks you are the dog's back. We all have needs, legitimate needs, but your spouse can't meet them all.'

'So I shouldn't expect any help from Helene?'

'Of course a wife should support her husband, and a husband, his wife. But none of us is perfect. We make mistakes. Some become so disillusioned or unfulfilled that they hop off like a flea to find another dog's back only to discover it's another flea.'

Last night at John's he'd wondered if he wouldn't be better off finding someone who appreciated him. But one night on John's cold, hard couch without Helene's warm body curled into his was enough to kill that thought. He'd just have to throw himself into his work and prove her wrong.

10

Dad slammed the door, slammed the fridge and slammed his beer on the kitchen table.

'Watch out. You'll smash that everywhere,' Mum growled. 'What's the matter with you, anyway?'

Mum and I were peeling the potatoes for tea. All our vegetables came from the back garden – potatoes and carrots, beans, corn and tomatoes in summer, and best of all, kumara. Mum and Dad stuck to the old ways with their vegetables, following the moon and stars for guidance on when to plant and when to harvest. It was almost Poututerangi – the time in March when the stars told them that the kumara was ready for eating. Mum would tell us kids how the old people had plenty of birds and fish from the bush and sea all year round but energy foods were scarce. The British brought bread, the Irish potatoes, the Chinese rice and the Italians pasta, but before they arrived Maori relied on kumara with its purple skin and sweet golden flesh. By summer time kumara stores were low and sometimes had even run out. So everyone looked forward to Poututerangi. I did too, even though I wasn't starving.

Tonight it was pudding that I was most looking forward to – strawberries and cream. In the warm afternoon sun I had picked all our sixteen precious strawberries, actually seventeen, but one 'accidentally' fell into my mouth, the delicious flavour bursting through my tastebuds. Mum had been saving them for a special occasion and tonight was it: today we got to own our house.

Mum dried her hands on her apron. 'You keep peeling, girl,' she whispered to me.

She walked over to Dad who was pacing round the room like one of those poor lions I once saw at the zoo – all restless and stuck in a cage. Mum pulled up two chairs and gently pushed him onto one. 'Sit down a minute.' Her plump, strong hand rested on his tensed shoulder. 'What's happened, my hoa rangatira?' Chiefly mate – it was Mum and Dad's special love code.

Dad patted Mum's hand then pulled the rent book out from his pocket and dropped it on the green formica table. 'This,' he flicked the book derisively, 'is a useless piece of … dirt.' I knew he wanted to swear but he never did in front of us kids. 'I told you they would do this to us. But I can't believe they've got away with it again. And we can't do a thing to stop it.' He put his head in his hands.

'Did you show them our rent book? How we haven't missed a payment in the whole six years? How we've paid every pound, shilling and sixpence right on time?' Mum asked.

'It did no bloody good,' Dad sighed. 'The bloke just said that the law had changed, that the whole rent-to-buy scheme was kicked out at some government meeting last week and now we can't buy our homes.'

'How can they do that?' Mum clenched her hands on her hips. Her eyes looked wet and wild at the same time.

'Like they always do, those bloody Pakehas.'

'They're not all bad.' Mum had calmed down. 'What about the Taylors up the hill and the Smiths and –'

'I know, I know. But they don't tell us where we can or can't live. They don't steal our land by making up some new law. And what can we do about it? How can we fight against the government? Upoko kohua!'

He thumped his fist on the table. It gave me such a fright I almost sliced my finger. I'd never heard him use that swear word before. I finished peeling the last potato and looked at my dad. His arms were strong and muscular. His legs were like smooth brown tree trunks, strong and sturdy.

'You could easily fight those people, Dad. You're much stronger than them.' I was really worried. My dad, who could dig a garden, fell a tree, paddle a waka, all without breaking a sweat, looked beaten.

He looked up at me, his brown eyes glistening. 'They use different weapons, Mere. If we're going to fight them we have to use the same weapons as them – the law.' Like the wind on the harbour he abruptly changed tack.

'Where's Rewiti? Did he catch any fish today?'

Mum blew her nose on a handkerchief and tucked it into her sleeve. 'We're having them for tea – two big kahawai. He came home feeling a bit sick. Probably got a chill from too much swimming at night. Go and see him. He's laying on his bed.'

Dad took another swig of his beer then headed to the bedroom. Mum picked up the knife and started chopping potatoes into quarters, then eights, then smaller.

'Mum, what are you doing?' I asked. 'Aren't those a bit small?'

Mum stared down absently at the diced spuds. She laughed but it was all choked up like Dad's mower when he tried to start it. 'Looks like I'm making potato salad!' Here Mere, you finish off, there's a good girl. I'll just go and check on Rewiti.'

My little sister kicked open the back door and staggered in under the weight of Charlie, our pet fox terrier. Her spindly arms struggled to contain his squirming body.

'What's wrong with Charlie?' I asked.

'There's blood on his face,' came her muffled reply. Charlie gave a final determined squirm straight out of Arahia's arms and out the door.

'He doesn't look too sick to me.'

'Yes he is. There's blood!' she insisted and raced out the door after the dog.

I chopped the last potato, dried my hands on my trousers and ran outside. She had disappeared.

'Charlie, Charlie, come back,' I heard her calling after the dog. I ran down the dirt track towards the beach. Arahia was chasing after Charlie. She dashed across Tamaki Drive, right in front of a car that swerved to miss her. I was puffing by the time I caught them up.

'He's got a bone or something in there.'

Arahia pointed at Charlie who was sniffing around a pile of driftwood heaped up in a corner of the beach. His head disappeared amongst the wood and seaweed. Then he started shaking something. The driftwood shifted and a tiny arm flopped out, no bigger than my little finger. I screamed. Arahia ran towards it.

'It's a baby! We've got to save it!'

I raced after her and grabbed her hand.

'It's too late. It's dead.'

It was more than dead, poor little mite. Except for the arm you wouldn't have known it was human. I felt sick.

'We've got to tell Dad. He'll want to give it a proper burial.' I put on my sternest voice. 'Charlie, come here.' Charlie looked up at me mournfully. I was ruining his fun. 'Come here now,' I ordered.

He reluctantly left the driftwood and the tiny dead baby. All three of us ran up the hill as fast as we could. I burst through the back door, panting for breath.

'Mum, Dad,' I cried. 'We found a baby on the beach. Charlie was eating it. He's got blood all over him. It's horrible.'

I was crying. Arahia was crying. Charlie put his tail between his legs like he knew he'd done something wrong. Mum and Dad came out of Rewiti's bedroom. They didn't look happy and I thought we were going to get into big trouble.

'Mum, Dad,' I started again.

Mum came over and gave us a hug. She was crying too.

'We heard you,' she said quietly.

Dad gave us a hug too. What was going on? Why weren't they mad at us? Dad heaved a deep breath.

'I'll go and sort it out right now. That bloody hospital, those bloody Pakehas.'

He stooped out the door looking just like Arahia had looked when she came in carrying Charlie, except he wasn't carrying anything that I could see.

The day we found the dead baby was the beginning of the blackest time in my life. Dad and Uncle Wiri buried the baby with all the others behind the sewerage pump shed. Their Pakeha bosses at the sewerage works always told them to burn any foetuses they found but there was no way a Maori would do that. It was not our way. Dad and Uncle Wiri would reverently wrap each tiny discarded body in cloth and carry it out the back to bury with the others. They prayed the karakia to send its little soul up to Cape Reinga at the very tip of the North Island and then on back to the ancestors in Hawaiki. I always wondered whether the souls of the little Pakeha babies went there too, or did they go somewhere else?

I soon found out why Mum and Dad weren't mad at us. It was Rewiti. He was really sick.

11

HELENE

Helene sat at a tiny wrought iron table tucked into a sunny corner of the café sipping iced water as she waited for Nicolette. She was always late. Her life was one hectic rush to fit as much into each day as possible. If she could squeeze in an extra meeting or phone call, she would. Did she ever sit and reflect on her life? Probably not. Perhaps that was the key to her success at work - and with men.

When she eventually swept into the café Nicolette looked as though she had just stepped out of *Vogue*. She wore a navy blue suit, the jacket half unbuttoned to reveal a lacy white camisole. Long tanned legs stretched to navy high-heeled shoes – European, of course.

Helene looked at her watch. It was five past one.. 'Hi, right on time!' she joked.

Nicolette laughed as she settled into the chair, crossing her legs at the ankles, just as she had learned at modelling school. 'Sorry about that, darling. My yoga class ran late.'

She touched her hair. 'Do you like it? Raphael streaked it a bit lighter than usual.'

'You look great.'

Helene glanced at the menu. 'Let's order now. Then we can relax and chat.'

'Great idea. I've been hanging out for a decent coffee all morning. The coffee machine at work is broken.'

Nicolette focussed on the menu for a moment, running her manicured fingernail down the laminated card.

'I think I'll have the smoked salmon salad. I'm cutting out carbs.'

'Nicolette! You don't need to diet. You look fabulous. Anyway that diet isn't all it's cracked up to be and it can be downright dangerous.'

'It's not really a diet at all – just cutting out bread, potato and biscuits. I still eat fruit and vegetables, and for breakfast I have a big bowl of muesli and yoghurt. Is that okay, doctor?'

'All right, all right. Just don't try anymore weird grapefruit, coconut or blue cheese diets.'

'Blue cheese? I haven't heard of that one.' Nicolette sounded interested.

'I'm just joking. There's no blue cheese diet.'

Helene rolled her eyes. Nicolette's diets lasted only a few weeks before she latched onto some new way to magically lose weight. The waiter arrived to take their orders. Nicolette's alluring smile was not wasted on him. Their low fat lattes and meals arrived in record time, along with more often than necessary top-ups of their water.

'A bit of flattery and a short skirt. It works every time!' Nicolette flicked her hair back with a sultry smile.

'Not that we needed it the other night at the restaurant. The service and food were fantastic. And Brad is gorgeous.'

Nicolette swirled a spoon in her coffee. 'Actually, I'm thinking of dumping him. He's a bit stifling, expecting me to attend all these rugby functions. I need some time to myself. Some freedom.' Her tongue toyed with the spoon and her eye caught the waiter's. That was sure to bring him panting to their table any minute now. 'Anyway, what's up with you? What's been happening?'

'Not much really, and that's just it. My life seems so boring compared with yours. I work all week and sit at home all weekend. We hardly go out and I can't remember the last time James and I had a proper conversation, you know, about feelings and stuff.'

'You could do a lot worse. Haven't you noticed the looks he gets? There are plenty of women who would snap him up in a moment if he wasn't already taken!'

'I guess so. He's charming when we are out but when we get home it is back to the daily grind. I'm only thirty-two. I shouldn't be stuck in a domestic rut at this age. I'm scared that this it for the rest of my life.'

'Perhaps you need a bit of spice in your life, a bit of harmless flirting. A few hot men to take notice of you and remind you how great you look.'

'I am not the type to hang around bars waiting for some stray man to chat me up.'

'Of course not, darling. You need to do what I do. Think about what you want and put it out to the universe.'

'Put it out to the universe?'

'I do it all the time. It really works.' She lowered her voice. 'You know, I did it with Brad.'

'Really?'

'Absolutely. I just imagined myself with a famous rugby player. Sort of like putting in your request for what you want. Then I put the vibes out to the universe to provide it for me. Within a week I had met Brad at a function and voila!'

'But it hasn't lasted.'

Nicolette blinked like a deer caught in headlights. 'I didn't specify long-term!' She pulled a tube of lip gloss from her hand-bag and dabbed it on her lips, refreshing the already immaculate red lipstick. 'Just give it a go. You've nothing to lose. Imagine some nice man bumping into you in the street, asking you to dinner, making you feel special. How long has it been since you felt like that? You work so hard helping all those sick people. You need to do something for yourself. You deserve it.'

'I guess I could try it out. But what about James?'

'Let's face it, Helene. You have only two choices: either put up with a boring marriage where the love will slowly drain away or take control and start searching for some happiness. If James finds out, so much the better. There's nothing like a bit of competition to shock a man into making an effort.'

'I could certainly do with a bit of that.'

Nicolette picked a cherry tomato from her plate and popped it carefully between her glossed lips. 'You've always achieved everything you set your mind to in your career. Now it is time to take control of your relationship. Decide what you want, put it out to the universe and it will give it to you.'

They chatted on while Helene's mind sifted through images of men she had known. It finally settled on Steve, her boyfriend from medical school. She hadn't thought about him in years. After Nicolette had rushed back to work Helene sat a moment longer, conjuring images of Steve in her mind. Then, feeling rather ridiculous, she whispered under her breath, 'Okay, universe. Here's Steve. I put him, or someone like him, out to you. Bring him to me.' Instantly she felt something brush past the side of her face, like a rush of wind except that she was sitting indoors. She tossed her head as if to shake away the uneasy feeling that descended upon her.

12

It was four in the morning. The sky was clear. The sea was icy. It gripped my lungs, forcing me to gasp just the way I used to when Rewiti sat on me punching my arm while I begged him to stop. Usually I deserved it. I liked to spy on him and his friends, hiding in the bushes and eavesdropping. Boy, was I in big trouble if he caught me. But it was worth it to see his handsome friends clowning around. I might even learn some new swear words. I swallowed a sob and almost a mouthful of brown sludge. My heart thudded in my chest. Not from exertion – I was a strong swimmer – but from fear. Being bashed up by my brother was nothing compared with what would happen if I got caught.

Like a stingray, I glided through the water in strong, silent breaststroke. Fear and a bit of cold water wasn't going to beat me. I held my head high and steady, carefully balancing a box of matches wrapped in a scrap of old sugar sack. Moonlight shimmered across the ripples, illuminating the way to my target.

I grabbed the side of the boat, hauled myself up and glanced around. Certain there was no one on board, I grabbed what I could find – a few rags, a grubby shirt, some ripped shorts. I searched for the spare petrol can and dragged it with the rags into the cabin. Dousing the rag pile with petrol, I splashed the rest around the seats, the steering wheel, across the floor and over the deck. I lit a match, dropped it on the rag pile and ran, diving into the sea. Ravenous flames roared across the deck. I kicked hard, head down, arms whirling through the water as fast as I could away from the crackling orange fire ball.

As soon as it was shallow enough to stand I ran, stumbling, across the cold, dark sand towards the flax bushes that separated the beach from the road. Hidden in the frosty, dew-laden flax were my long pants and jacket. Shaking with adrenaline and cold, I peeled off my dripping shorts and t-shirt and pulled on the damp clothes, my frozen fingers struggling with the zip. My breath wheezed out like an old steam train in the winter air. I cupped my hands over my mouth and forced myself to breathe slowly in and out, in and out. My lungs gradually relaxed. The wheezing stopped. I fumbled in the flax again and retrieved my nanny's large flax kete, into which I had stuffed a thick grey blanket. I wrapped it round myself and sat staring at the flames.

'This is for you, Rewiti, and for you, Nanny.' I ran my fingers over the smooth flax of the kete. Nanny had cut the harekeke and woven this basket just for me. I felt her love, her aroha, through it. I drew my knees up to my chest and wrapped the blanket tighter around myself. Only then did I allow myself to cry. Great heaving sobs. The grief of the past few months poured out of me like a breached dam.

'Rewiti, you were meant to live. You were the smart one, the strong one who caught all the fish and swam faster than all the others. How could you die?'

I still couldn't believe it. Any moment I expected to see him come sauntering up the hill with a catch of fish, laughing with his mates. Sometimes I still heard his voice.

'I did this for you.'

Rewiti would have done the same for me, shown those Pakeha fellas they couldn't use the bay like a car park for their boats. Who did they think they were – burning the village, polluting the fishing grounds, killing the children? Rewiti wasn't the first to die from swimming in the putrid water. Waimate, the elders called it, the water that makes you sick. Once the red spots came up on your tummy everyone knew there wasn't much hope. The tohunga's powers didn't work on these Pakeha sicknesses. And those Pakeha doctors couldn't be trusted.

With a splintering crash the boat's mast toppled into the sea. The fire still crackled orange in the early morning dark. Black smoke shrouded the frosty bay. It smelled like burnt toast. I wiped away my hot tears and snotty nose with the back of my hand. The damp blanket was little comfort in this pre-dawn June morning. My bare feet were frozen. Better get home before anyone noticed I wasn't there. I stuffed the blanket back into my precious kete, crossed Tamaki Drive and ran up the road to the sleeping state houses perched on the hill overlooking the bay and a smouldering skeleton of a boat.

'Mere, wake up.' Arahia shook me awake. 'You'd better get up quick. Mum's calling you.'

I rubbed my blurry eyes and swung my legs over the side of the bed. The cold wooden floor jolted me awake. 'What time is it?' I yawned.

Arahia bounced up and down on my bed, her long, un-brushed hair flying around her face. 'It's eight o'clock. Dad's gone again. I think Mum wants you to go find him.'

I groaned. Now that I was the eldest Mum relied on me a lot, especially when it came to Dad. Everything was different without Rewiti, like there was a big hole in the family. Mum was smoking non-stop. Arahia had started sucking her thumb again.

But Dad had changed the most. He was like Arahia's teddy bear with all the stuffing pulled out. You couldn't talk to him. He wasn't really listening. The only thing he listened for was Rewiti's voice, his laugh. The dog would scratch at the door or it might rattle in the wind and he'd be out of his seat, swinging open the door. 'Rewiti, is that you?' Then his head would sag, his shoulders slump like a heavy bag had dropped on him, and he'd disappear for a few hours or sometimes the whole day. He always came home at night to Mum, his hoa rangatira, his comfort. Arahia and I would lie in bed trying to sleep through Mum and Dad's broken sobs, which pierced the thin walls and my heart.

'Where did you go last night?' Arahia asked, still bouncing on the bed. 'Your bed was empty when I got up for a pee. What were you doing?'

'Nothing.' I glared at her.

'I'll tell Mum.'

I grabbed her tangled hair. 'Don't you dare or I'll pull your hair right out of your head.' I yanked hard.

'Ow, let go, let go,' Arahia screamed.

'Promise you'll keep your mouth shut?'

'I promise!'

I let go and headed for the kitchen, leaving Arahia on the bed rubbing her head. Mum was pacing up and down the kitchen, sucking the life out of a cigarette.

'Your dad didn't come home last night.'

She looked terrible, her blood shot eyes sunken in deep, dark rings and her faded blue dressing gown drooping open, inside-out, over crumpled clothes. She stubbed her cigarette butt out in the overflowing ashtray and picked up the almost empty pack. 'He always comes home. Something must have happened. I've rung Uncle Wiri. He's not there. You stay here with Arahia. I'm going out to find him.'

She shoved another cigarette in her mouth and tried to strike a match. I looked out the window. Rain battered the thin glass. I looked at Mum's worn grey slippers scuffing the floorboards in distracted circles.

'I'll go look for him, Mum. You stay here in case he comes home.'

Mum came over and wrapped her arms around me, hugging me fiercely.

'You're a good girl, Mere. What would I do without you?' She started to cry. 'Put Dad's oilskin on. It will keep you dry.' She cried harder. Dad would be soaking wet, wherever he was.

Like a black shadow I headed down the hill, trying not to trip over the oilskin that dragged along the muddy track. It would have been easier walking down the road but Dad might have fallen or got lost on the hillside. I stepped carefully, trying not to slip in the mud. The rain blew in sheets across the bay, hitting me in the face whenever I peered up to see where I was going. I could just see the outline of the burnt out boat. No one seemed to have noticed it yet. Where could Dad be? He'd gone drinking with Uncle Wiri like he always did on

Saturday night. But where did he go after that? My gaze swept inland from the bay, across the beach, up over the road and down to the urupa where Rewiti was buried. The urupa and a quarter acre was all that was left of our land, our home. Dad was always going to Rewiti's grave. Maybe he was there.

The rain stopped just as I entered the urupa. Thank goodness. It was scary enough walking amongst all the dead ancestors without it raining too.

'Dad?' My voice sounded so loud in the deserted, gloomy graveyard. I headed straight for Nanny's grave, the one with the huge headstone giving her a place of honour in death just as she had been in life.

'E kui, where's your son? Where's Dad?'

Of course dead people couldn't speak. But who else could I ask? I glanced at Rewiti's shiny new grave, covered with flowers from Mum's garden and his favourite childhood toy – a battered red fire truck. He wouldn't get a headstone until next year. Perhaps I would be able to look at his grave by then. Right now it was too painful. I focussed on my nanny's headstone.

Maimai aroha
Na to whanau katoa
Haere ki Te Kai Hanga
Whatu ngaro he whenua
Toitu he mana
Haere ra

Loving wife, mum, nanny and aunty.
Safe in the arms of Jesus.
The land may go but your love, your example and your strength live on.

March 1952

That stinking Pakeha government murdered not only Rewiti but also my beloved nanny. I was a little kid then, only seven or eight, but I remember every moment of those dreadful last few months of

Nanny's life. After Dad dragged her from her burning whare she never spoke again. Every day I sat for hours beside her as she lay curled up, refusing to eat. I would stroke her hand, willing life into her. At first her hand was plump and warm but over the weeks it became bony and cold as the life slowly seeped out of her.

'It's no use, e moko,' my granddad would comfort me with tears in his eyes. 'She's marched to Wellington, spoken to parliament, written to the leaders, prayed, cried, shouted for justice. But when some insignificant civil servant marches onto your land waving a piece of paper that says he's allowed to burn your home and evict you from the last vestige of land he hasn't already stolen, you know you've lost the battle.'

I could hardly bear to hear my strong, stately koro speak with such defeat.

'Let her go to God, Mere. It's someone else's turn to fight. Perhaps yours.'

I remember gripping onto Nanny's hand while my koro gripped mine. It felt like he was willing his strength, his mana, into me.

Five years later, as we clustered around Rewiti, stroking his dank hair, clutching his feverish hand to stop him clawing his skin to shreds, and soothing his delirious typhoid cries with our own I vowed that I would fight.

Two seagulls swooped over my head, squawking as they chased each other. They alighted on the tiny church, dilapidated but still standing next to the urupa, then hopped through a glassless window. Could Dad be in there? The heavy wooden door creaked as I pushed it open and stepped inside. The winter wind blew through the windows but at least it was warmer than outside. I peeled off my sodden oilskin and draped it over a pew. Damp steam rose from the checked flannel lining.

'Dad, are you in here?' I spoke tentatively, reverently. God was in here. I sure hoped Dad was too. The seagulls strutted up and down a pew seat, splashing in a puddle of water.

'I'm here, daughter.' Dad raised his head and uncurled himself. He'd been asleep right next to the altar. I ran to where he sat and flung my arms around him.

'Are you alright, Dad? Mum's really worried about you. Why didn't you come home last night?'

He buried his head in my shoulder and sighed a great, heaving sigh. He smelt like Uncle Wiri's house after a party – spilt beer and stale smoke.

'I wanted to see Rewiti. It was raining so hard, I thought I'd come in here. I must have fallen asleep.' He gently released my arms from around him and took hold of both my hands. His eyes were red like Mum's. 'Your hands are like ice blocks.'

'So are yours. We'd better get home and see Mum.'

The heavy church door creaked open, letting in a shaft of light. Mrs Taylor, the old lady who played the organ, stood shaking the rain off her umbrella.

'My, my, you two are keen,' she twittered, looking at us still kneeling at the altar.

Dad squirmed. 'We were just leaving.'

'Please don't leave on account of me,' Mrs Taylor implored, her tone more serious. 'In fact, you are an answer to my prayers, you and the rain stopping. We're having church on the beach this morning. I know it's the middle of winter but the minister telephoned me on Wednesday and insisted. Goodness knows why! So we have to move the organ down there. Would you be so kind as to help me and Ted?'

She stood in the doorway beaming like a round, pink ball in her bright woollen coat and sensible brown shoes. All the kids loved Mrs Taylor. She was always smiling, especially when she banged out the Sunday School songs on the portable pedal organ. And her coat pockets were usually full of sweets that she gave to the kids who sang the loudest. Sunshine now streamed through the windows, flooding the church with light and warmth. I felt my sadness and fear evaporate, and glanced at Dad. He looked much better too. He didn't smile but when he stood up he looked sort of lighter.

'Sure, I can help you, Mrs Taylor. In fact, I might even stay for the service.' He patted me on the back. 'Run home and tell Mum I'm fine. Tell her to come down to church. I'll meet you there.'

'Thank you so much,' Mrs Taylor beamed even brighter. 'Ted

will be over to help shortly. He's just talking to the police on the beach. There's quite a crowd gathering. Did you see that boat out there? Burned to smithereens! I hope no one was on board.'

I hurried out of the church, smiling politely at Mrs Taylor and holding my breath. I ducked through the grave stones out the back, away from the beach. At the first muddy puddle outside the urupa I crouched down and washed my hands, cleansing myself from the dead. It wasn't clean water but it would have to do. The tap was on the beach side of the urupa and there was no way I was going near those cops.

***

A small crowd gathered on the beach for the church service. Some sat on folding chairs that threatened to topple in the soft sand. Others sat on the sand hills covered with flax, in exactly the same spot I had been five or six hours before. I tried to focus on what the minister was saying while glancing furtively at the two policemen clambering around on what was left of the boat.

'Do you think they found a body?' Mum whispered to her friend, Aunty Joan.

Aunty knew all the gossip in Auckland. She and Mum spent every Tuesday and Thursday afternoon playing canasta, drinking syrupy tea and discussing who was doing what. As soon as I walked in the door after school they would hastily stub out their cigarettes, open a window and ply me with fresh baked rewena bread or pikelets lathered with butter. There was nothing better than coming home to that cosy kitchen filled with cigarette smoke, delicious food and best of all, Mum's hearty laughter.

'There's no body,' Aunty replied, her hand hiding her mouth while she looked at the minister, her face feigning great interest in whatever he was saying. 'I heard the police say they found the owner passed out in one of "those places" in the city. You know what I mean.' She winked at Mum and gave a coquettish toss of her head.

'No! Really?' If it had been summer, Mum would have swallowed a fly with her mouth wide open like that.

'He does it all the time,' Aunty continued. 'Haven't you noticed his boat parked up here in the bay every weekend? It's been going on all year as far as I can tell. A few folks around here have been getting pretty mad about it. I reckon someone's had enough, decided to scare him off.'

I dug my toes in the sand and kept quiet.

'I'm guessing that the police won't try too hard to catch the culprit.'

Would she ever shut up or at least change the subject? My toe scraped something sharp. I reached down and dug out a beer bottle top, pretending not to listen to Aunty's speculations.

Aunty put on her bossy voice. 'If he's smart he'll let the whole thing drop before they haul the boat out of the water and find something that will get him in real trouble.'

A flock of seagulls landed on the beach. One tried to hop on Mrs Taylor's organ. She waved it off and smiled at the minister, who was just finishing his sermon. He had paused for a moment, stroking his beard as though in great thought. The silence drew everyone's attention. He looked around at each person as if he wanted to run over and hug them. There were tears in his eyes.

'If there's one thing you remember from today, remember these words from Romans chapter twelve.' He spoke with an intensity I had never heard before.

Do not repay anyone evil for evil … Do not take revenge, my friends, but leave room for God's wrath, for it is written: 'It is mine to avenge; I will repay,' says the Lord.

The words hammered at my heart.

In doing this you will heap burning coals on his head.

Burning coals. That's exactly how my face felt. It was fine for him to tell everyone not to take revenge. He wouldn't know what it was like. As if he had read my thoughts, the minister continued, his voice shaking like he was trying not to cry.

'You may be thinking "Who's this Pakeha telling us not to pay back those who have hurt us? He wouldn't understand." But it's not me who says these things, it's God – the God of the Bible, the God of justice, who loves each one of you.'

My face burned, my heart hammered. I felt ill.

13

Helene arrived home from work early to find Mere kneeling beside the garden, weeding.

'Hi, Mere. You don't have to do that, you know.'

Mere looked up from under her straw hat and grinned. 'I hope you don't mind. Gardening is therapeutic, helps me clear my mind. I've been writing all morning and need a break.'

'Are you sure? It's certainly a great help to us.'

'It's the least I can do while I'm here.' She coughed, then pushed herself to her feet and rubbed the dirt off her hands. 'That's better. What are you doing home so early? Is no one sick today?'

Helene laughed. 'It's my afternoon off.'

'Well, I need a cool drink. I've baked rewena. You must try some.'

A warm hint of freshly baked bread mingled with the earthy scent of the garden.

'I wondered what that delicious smell was. How do you make it?'

'It's a little like sour dough – made with fermented potato water.' She patted her stomach. 'There's only one problem with it; once you start eating, it's hard to stop. Come on inside. I've made myself hungry just talking about it.'

Helene followed Mere into the guest house. She felt drawn to her by some emotional magnet that she could not comprehend.

'So how's the writing going?' she asked as Mere pulled off her gardening gloves and washed her hands. A computer sat on the table surrounded by orderly piles of paper and a stack of bound official looking documents. Next to the computer lay an open Bible.

'I've written a couple of chapters. The actual writing is easy but sometimes it's difficult to drag all those memories up from the past.'

She filled two glasses with cordial, ice and water and cut two generous slices from a large, round loaf of bread, smearing them with a thin layer of butter. 'You can't eat rewena without butter. It would be like eating eggs without salt. I haven't put too much on, not like I used to.' Her mischievous chuckle caught in her throat and changed to a hacking cough. She gripped the back of a chair to steady herself, her eyes watery from the exertion.

Helene stepped towards her to help but Mere waved her away.

'It's all right dear, just an annoying tickle in my throat.' She straightened up and smiled. 'See, I'm right as rain.'

Helene picked up the glasses of cordial. 'Let's sit out on the balcony. It's lovely and warm in the sun and it might help clear up your cough.'

As they walked across to the main house Helene took a sip of her drink. 'Ginger cordial. My favourite. It's made here in Queensland, you know.'

Mere followed her up the steps to the balcony. 'It's delicious. My grandkids would love it. I must see if we can get it in New Zealand.'

'So when do you need to return?' They settled into comfortable chairs and placed the bread and drinks on the wooden table.

'I've booked my ticket for early next month but it's flexible, just in case I need to go sooner. We'll see. A man sets his plans but the Lord directs his steps.'

What on earth did she mean by that? The bemusement must have shown on Helene's face.

'It sounds a bit cryptic but it's true. We make our plans and set goals but because the Lord loves us and knows what is best for us, he might steer us in a different direction.'

'Are you saying that it's a waste of time to plan and set goals?'

'Not at all dear. It's important to have a direction in life. But God's ways are often quite different from ours and how you achieve your goal may not always be the obvious way. He's very innovative like that, and it always works out better in the long run.'

'How can you be sure it's better?' asked Helene.

'There's a verse in the Bible that says: *I know the plans I have for you, plans to give you hope and a future*. Over the years I have come to believe it.'

'My friend and I were just talking about this. If you want something you just put it out to the universe. If it's good for you, it will happen and if it's not, it won't.'

Mere's smile faded. 'That depends on who you are speaking to.'

'I didn't think I was speaking to anyone. Isn't it just positive thinking?'

'It's a little more than positive thinking and that's why it's good to know who you are really asking.'

Later that evening Helene stood at the stove stirring a lemon risotto. Her mind moved in time with the spoon, around and around, back and forth. The more she thought about it, the less clear it became. Mere made plans but allowed God to have the final say, as though she were a child needing parental guidance. Helene winced at the thought. Nicolette made plans and put them out to the universe for some sort of cosmic help. That seemed harmless enough although Mere hadn't liked it. She topped up her glass of sauvignon blanc and took a sip, still stirring the risotto. Most likely her little universe experiment at the café would come to nothing, Mere would soon return to New Zealand, and she could stop having these weird thoughts. She poured more hot stock into the risotto and heard the front door click shut. James trudged into the kitchen dumping his briefcase on the kitchen table.

'Don't put that there! We have to eat off that table.'

'Welcome home too.' James removed the bag to the floor.

Helene kept stirring but dropped her voice to a calmer tone. 'It's just that I hate it when you dump your bag there.'

James grabbed a can of beer from the fridge and took a long swig. 'Boy, I needed that! The receptionist was sick today and I've got a couple of clients breathing down my neck wanting their projects finished yesterday.'

'Couldn't you have got a temp in for the day? That's what we do at our practice.'

James leaned against the wall and took another swig of beer. 'I suppose so. Maybe I'll do that next time.'

'Next time! Are you expecting her to do this a lot?'

'She's pregnant. When she does come in, she spends half the time flopping on her desk and the other half running to the toilet.'

'What if it continues like this for the next six months?' Helene asked. 'Why don't you employ a casual to cover the days she can't do?'

'Helene, stop telling me how to run my own business. I'm taking care of it and I've thought through all that. Can't I tell you anything without you trying to solve it for me?'

'I was only trying to help.' He was so touchy these days.

'Well they sounded more like criticisms to me.' James retreated to the lounge and switched on the news. Helene turned back to her risotto just as it started to catch and burn on the bottom. Now there was a lesson: never mix risotto with arguments.

14

How much longer would this go on? I wiped a calloused hand across my forehead and rested my wheezing bulk on the rusty garden fork. My gaze swept across the panorama below. To my left stood the city centre – short, squat and tall sleek buildings sandwiched together, their stainless steel and glass shimmering in the afternoon heat. Just beyond the Auckland Harbour Bridge arched from the city to the North Shore. I watched the streaming cars and trucks, remembering a very different scene just a few years earlier. As Derek bounced on my hip and the other kids jumped up and down, we had done our best to spot their dad amongst the hundreds of Maori marching over the bridge on their long hikoi from Cape Reinga to Wellington. I remembered the chants: 'Not one more acre of Maori land', 'Give it back', 'Honour the Treaty'. The Maori Land March had achieved much, but not enough.

Directly opposite Bastion Point, a few short kilometres across the harbour, was the sleepy suburb of Devonport, surrounded by beach and tucked between two grassy hills. The stark grey battlements built in World War Two to defend Auckland against possible invasion still scarred the brilliant green hillsides. Across the harbour entrance was Rangitoto Island. Like a stretched out triangle, perfectly symmetrical, it looked so close I could almost touch it. In front of the island a ferry cut a white trail through the deep blue of the harbour. A light scatter of yachts and fishing boats dotted the sea in between distant green islands of rich farmland and native bush. This was the view that the thieving government was trying to get its dirty hands on. This was why I was digging kumara in the scorching afternoon heat and not greeting the kids with pikelets and raspberry cordial when they arrived home, hot and tired after school.

From the far end of the kumara patch Dad called to me: 'Hey, Mere, you got all those kumara dug up?'

'Yeah, that's the last of 'em done.'

I swung the garden fork onto my shoulder and trudged over to Dad. He stood, sturdy brown legs astride a soil-clumped hoe, surveying their work. Gnarled purple tubers lay scattered across the ground, drying out before they were gathered and stored.

'You want a drink?' He offered me a large, half-empty bottle of Fanta. The fizzy bubbles stung my parched throat but it was worth it for the sweet orange flavour. I took another gulp.

'If those fullas up at the camp are so keen to get a feed of kumara they should have come down here and helped,' I grumbled. 'They keep saying they can't wait to eat them but when it's time to dig them up they say they're too busy.'

Dad smiled, his face crinkling into layers of brown withered wrinkles. The past year of working in the garden, providing food and a way to keep the protestors occupied, had weathered his face but strengthened his body. He smiled a lot more these days.

'Patience. That's what they need. That's what we all need. Tell those fullas to come and get them in a couple of days when they're dried out. They can store them in that shed next to their precious snooker table. And then they can wait.'

Waiting. That was what kumara needed. You waited to harvest so they would be nice and big. Then you waited for them to dry out. Then you waited some more to let them sweeten up and heal themselves from the accidental assault of a garden fork or careless muddy boot. If you wanted the biggest, sweetest, golden kumara, you waited. Last year we had waited even longer to harvest. Mind you, we didn't plant the three thousand donated plants until February. It was three months too late. I smiled as I recalled what Dad's friend had said to him:

'I knew you were dumb but I didn't know you were stupid. If them plants grow, I'll eat my hat.'

There was no way that kumara planted so late should grow, but by May we had a bumper crop of big, fat, golden kumara. It was a miracle. Kumara were like gold but for the protestors camped on Bastion Point, as well as all the manuhiri who swelled the numbers each time the elders called a hui, the expensive vegetable was on the menu breakfast, lunch and dinner.

'It's the Lord blessing us and our cause,' Dad had insisted. To his mate: 'E hoa, you'd better start eating your hat!'

I wiped my hands on my cavernous black skirt. 'I'd better get over to the kitchen and help out. We're cooking up that pig that someone dropped off yesterday – special treat. Are you all right here by yourself, Dad?'

''Course I am,' Dad growled. 'Gives me time to think.' His voice softened. 'Thanks for helping out today. You're a good girl, Mere.' He stretched a wiry arm around my shoulder and squeezed me to his side. He could still give a mean hug. 'I'll see you at tea later, ay?'

I plodded through the garden and across the metal road to the camp. A couple of the camp dogs ran over, sniffing around my sweaty legs. Since having the kids I'd got a lot bigger. People listened to you when you were big – better than being skinny – but in this heat, with the sweat pooling in the folds around my stomach and running between my chafing thighs, I wished I was a bit smaller. Sighing, I dismissed the thought. There were plenty more important things to worry about, like holding the household together while Doug was away, trying to pay the mounting bills, and keeping those boys in line. They were kicking a rugby ball on the rough grass that sloped from the camp all the way down to the gun battlements standing sentry in the cliffs above Tamaki Drive and the harbour. In the distance I saw Derek diving to tackle his cousin. If I let them, they'd spend all their time playing around the camp. Getting them to do their school work was like getting the government to keep its promises.

'Hey, you kids. Get up here now,' I shouted, hands planted on my hips. My booming voice halted their game. All four heads turned. They kicked the ball towards me and came running. 'Have youse all done your homework?' I demanded.

Derek stared at his toes while his ten-year-old cousin Danny spoke up for the guilty group. 'Aw Aunty, we haven't got any today.'

I drew myself up to my full, intimidating breadth. 'Don't tell lies, boy. I know you have reading and times tables every day.'

Danny wiped a grubby hand across his hot face and sniffed. His knees were black with dirt, his tight, white shorts smeared green with grass stains. Derek didn't look much better.

'Please, Aunty. Can't we just finish our game?' He threw the ball at Derek – a straight pass to the stomach – making him look up.

'Yeah, Mum. We'll go do our homework after that. Promise.'

Their carefree, hopeful faces pleaded with me. They didn't get it; how important school was for their future. The tribe needed to make sure they brought up the next generation right. That meant giving them a good education in both the Pakeha way and their Maori traditions. I looked at them jiggling around, itching to get back to their game, and put on my most fearsome frown.

'Okay, you can go play. But tomorrow you'd better get straight over to Aunty Jean's after school for homework help. And if I find out you weren't there, you'll get a good hiding.'

'Okay, Mum.'

'Thanks, Aunty.'

The boys took off like fish released from the net. They knew my bark was worse than my bite. If only Doug were home. One word from their father and they leaped into action.

I headed towards the kitchen and the mouth-watering smell of roasting pork. It was all action. People were peeling potatoes. Others were cutting them into chunks and tossing them onto enormous trays, dotted with dripping, ready for roasting. Still others were peeling and slicing apples into an industrial sized pot. Roast pork wasn't roast pork without crackling and apple sauce. Since Doug had brought back those ten cases of apples from Hastings we had eaten apple almost every day – apple pie, apple cake and stewed apple topped with cream and custard. Now Doug was away again, up north this time, drumming up support for the cause. People were so generous. If they couldn't get down here to camp on Bastion Point they provided support by donating mattresses, building materials, money or food. I grabbed a long metal spoon and stood over the stove stirring a huge pot of stewed apple. My skirt clung limply to my legs, gathering smoke and ash. No one wore their best clothes around here, especially not if they were on cooking duty.

We were just getting ready to dish up when Derek ran into the kitchen, crying.

'Mummy, the chickens got me. Look!' He twisted around to show me his bleeding leg.

'They ain't no chickens, boy,' one of the young men laughed as he pulled the sizzling roast meat from the oven, his tattoos bulging. Mouth-watering wafts of hot pork crackling filled the room. He wiped his hands on his blue overalls. 'There's no way you'll see an egg coming out of one of those. Whoever gave us those tyrant roosters might have meant well but they sure need to learn the difference between a male and female.'

I enveloped Derek in my arms. He snuggled into my soft rolls. The roosters ruled the camp with their dawn crowing and vicious beaks. I rubbed the blood off his leg. It wasn't too serious.

'How about you take my umbrella? That gives them a good fright.'

Derek, fully recovered after a few moments of motherly attention, squirmed free.

'Nah, Mum. It looks stink. I'll find a stick to whack 'em with.' He raced off out the door.

'Don't you boys go too far. It's almost teatime.'

'Sure, Mum.'

Everyone gathered around the trestle tables laid out in front of the kitchen. Hot, steaming vegetables, glistening with butter, thickly sliced roast pork and crackling, and stainless steel bowls of apple sauce were lined up in the serving area ready to go. There weren't too many people at camp tonight so we would all be able to eat together rather than in the two or three sittings we sometimes had. Father Michael stood up to say the karakia. No one was allowed to start eating until they had thanked God for the food. We stood with heads bowed, some more reverently than others. Dad, the gardening grime and sweat washed from his face, stood next to Father Michael. You could tell that those two really believed. They prayed as though they were actually talking to a real person and at the end they kept their eyes shut for a few moments longer, as though listening for a reply. I glanced up in time to see Derek sneaking a piece of pork and glared. He raised his arms in mock innocence, mouthing the word 'What?' the piece of meat skilfully concealed in the side of his mouth. I knew that trick. I had done it plenty of times myself. And who could blame him? There was nothing better than roast pork.

I lined up behind Aunty Jean's nephew, who was elbowing his mate beside him, both giggling like school boys. They were part of the 'rat patrol' – the group that patrolled Bastion Point at night, ensuring no government bulldozers or other trespassers tried to sneak onto the land. He grabbed a plate off the pile and handed one to me.

'Here you go, Aunty.'

I took the plate and helped myself to a pile of roast pork and crackling.

'What are you two giggling about?'

'I was just saying how blessed we are,' he laughed. 'We have church in the morning, we have church before we have a feed and church every night. I have never been so blessed in my life!'

They cracked up laughing again.

'Yeah,' his mate agreed. 'And you're blessed it's not raining tonight so you don't end up in the mud on your fat bum.'

They shoved each other again like a couple of play-fighting puppies. A few pieces of meat toppled from their laden plates into the drooling jaws of the camp dogs.

I squeezed onto the wooden bench seat and picked up my knife and fork. Blessed? Were we blessed that the government had burnt our village? Were we blessed that Rewiti and so many others had died? Were we blessed that we had to camp up here right through the freezing, wet winter with the wind howling around the makeshift buildings? Were we blessed that we had no money because Doug had cut back his work days at the wharf so he could support the protest? And yet during this past year good things had happened. Dad had never been this content, not even before Rewiti died. The young kids didn't mope around with that hopeless look on their faces. They wanted to be around the camp all the time absorbing the history, the songs, the mana of a culture not entirely crushed by government greed. Yes, this Bastion Point stand had given the young ones a sense of purpose and pride. Perhaps we were being blessed. But how long would we have to wait? When and how would it ever end?

15

Dad paced slowly, thoughtfully, back and forth in front of the respectful crowd. Every night for the past five hundred and six days the people camped here on Bastion Point gathered in the meeting house called Te Arohanui to discuss the protest, to talk, to sing, to laugh and to pray. Some stood, some leaned against the muralled walls. The older ones sat on chairs while others relaxed on the mattresses scattered over the carpet.

'He pai te whenua, he pai hoki nga hua: If the land is good, what comes from the land is good.' He paused, allowing the words to sink in. 'I know you've heard me say this before when I've tried to get you lazy beggars to help in the garden.'

The crowd laughed. As if on cue a loud snore escaped from the flaccid mouth of a man lying sprawled across one of the donated mattresses, his blue track pants straining below a partially exposed bloated stomach. The woman sitting beside him punched his solid arm. 'Hey, that's you, ay.' He woke up with a yelp. The crowd laughed some more.

'Yeah, ya slacker. How come you disappear every time there's work to do?

We'd better give you an award for the best Houdini act, ay?'

Unperturbed by the friendly jibes the man patted his bulging tummy. 'My work is to appreciate the food all these beautiful ladies cook for us.' He grinned at the women around the room. A few of them rolled their eyes. Others laughed. The women who had just punched him leant over and smacked a lingering kiss on his lips.

'Yeah, you contribute in other ways.' The tin shed rattled with raucous laughter. Dad smiled and said nothing until the noise subsided. He started pacing back and forth again as he resumed speaking.

'Tonight the land I'm talking about is the land of our hearts. We've got to get our hearts right so what happens tomorrow is right.' The crowd went deadly quiet, their faces suddenly serious.

'Tomorrow the police are going to come up here with their trucks and batons and piece of paper from the court and try to kick us off our land.'

'Let 'em try,' muttered a pale thin lad pushing lank, greasy hair away from his bloodshot eyes. He punched his fist into his palm. The slouching group around him snarled in agreement. Dad looked directly at them. 'I have a special job for you fullas tomorrow. You will be our generals, in charge of our most important people, the kuia and kaumatua – our elders. Make sure they don't get hurt. Stand by them. Don't leave their side, no matter what happens. You are their protection.' The troublemakers fell silent, their fighting hands slipped to their sides and they stood a little taller.

Dad continued. 'Our ancestors were mighty warriors, tough, strong and smart. Tomorrow some of you will want to fight – it's in your blood to fight – but there's smart fighting and dumb fighting. A true warrior fights smart. He uses his brain. He knows his enemy. Tomorrow our enemy is not the army trucks or the police, it's a piece of paper. What happens if you punch a piece of paper? Nothing. For the past five hundred and six days we have said we will fight the government their way – with the law. We're not changing tomorrow. Like our mighty warrior ancestors we will be disciplined. We will not react. We will be strong. It's easy to throw a punch but this is not a physical battle. It's a battle of the law, of justice. We will keep our dignity, our mana. This is our land and we will peacefully remain on it, no matter what.'

Assenting murmurs rose from around the room. Dad stopped

pacing. He reached under his chair and pulled out a well-used Bible, holding it high above his head. 'And we will pray all night – to the God of justice. We will ask Him to fight for us, just as he did for Gideon, for Joshua and for Moses.'

The praying, the singing, the speeches went on for hours. I dozed a little. It was around four in the morning when I stepped outside. I breathed in the crisp autumn air. It curled around my asthmatic lungs, threatening to send them into spasm, but it was invigorating after the cloying human heat within the wharenui. I looked up at the stars. Those very stars had guided my ancestors here to New Zealand one thousand years ago. And when the European newcomers sailed in on their ships eight hundred years later we had willingly shared it. But Maori were still the kaitiaki, the caretakers of the land. This Bastion Point stand was about preserving the land not just for our tribe, but for all the people of New Zealand, whether they realised it or not.

I wrapped my cloak tightly against the biting breeze, my fingers caressing the greenstone fishing hook and metal sinker hanging around my neck. Both were Rewiti's. A year after Rewiti's death, at the unveiling of his headstone, Dad had given me the smooth, polished greenstone hook.

'This is for you, Mere.' His eyes had glistened with grief. 'Hold it close to your heart. Your great-grandfather made it. He called it Rongo because he was a man of peace. May it give you peace as it has for me during this past year.'

Since that day, almost twenty years earlier, the cool, soothing stone had nestled on my chest. I rubbed it again. It would protect me tomorrow. On a shorter cord, above the greenstone, hung the sinker I had stolen from Rewiti's fishing line not long after he'd made it. He had been mad for days, searching for it. It was his best sinker but I hadn't stolen it to use it. I stole it to remember. Rewiti had made it from a piece of roof on that terrible day when the whole village was burnt to the ground. Now, twenty-seven years later, here we were, yet again, preparing to face eviction from our own land by the money-hungry government. But this time was different. No longer were we on our own. People from all around New Zealand and the world had come to support our cause over the past year and a half. Thanks to the media, this time there would be no secrets and no lies.

'Fancy a cuppa?' Mum hobbled out from the kitchen with two cups of steaming, milky tea. 'I've put plenty of sugar in. We need our energy tonight.'

She passed me a cup and plonked down on a home-made wooden bench propped against the building. She patted the space next to her. 'Come and sit next to me, my daughter.'

I balanced myself on the narrow seat. It wobbled under our weight.

'You should be asleep, Mum, you're not well.' I patted her knee. 'How's your leg?'

Mum pulled up one leg of her trousers. Even in the dark I could see the necrosing wound on her shin.

'It's not too bad,' she replied.

'Looks bad to me.'

Who would have thought that such a little scratch could turn into that? A medical student who spent his weekends at the camp had said she might have diabetes and should probably see a doctor.

'How about I walk you back to Arahia's place? Get a few hours' sleep before whatever happens this morning.'

Mum shook her head. 'I'm too tired to walk. Anyway, my place is here tonight, supporting your father and making the tea.' She sipped her drink and gazed out at the harbour. 'Your father was right all those years ago. He knew what the government was up to, bribing us off our land with new state houses. We used to fight about it all the time. I wanted the modern things – a new house, electricity, a flush toilet – but he knew better. I've learnt my lesson. This time I'm not arguing with him; I'm standing by him.'

She stretched out her sore leg. '… even if it hurts.'

We sat together, mother and daughter, sipping our tea and watching the first traces of morning seep across the sky.

***

'Get down on your knees and be prepared to pray for peace!' The booming voice of the 'pistol packing' preacher, as he was known, thundered out from the meeting house. I rose stiffly from the bench and looked at my watch. It was five am. I must have dosed off. Mum was gone; probably back in the kitchen serving tea. Like the suspended stillness after a gunshot, the meeting house was suddenly silent. I peeked through the door. The sight that greeted me made me want to laugh and cry at the same time. Everyone was kneeling on the floor with head bowed: Maori, non-Maori, the women, the men, the elders, the rebelliously tattooed 'generals' who had probably never prayed before in their lives, even the self-avowed communists kneeled, heads bowed, praying to a god they didn't believe in. The air felt heavy and still, like a peaceful blanket had gently settled over the people. I bowed my head also and listened to Dad and the 'pistol packing' preacher as they cried out to God for justice and peace. We prayed until breakfast.

Breakfast was subdued, not the usual jokes and laughter. Everyone knew that this was probably the last meal we would eat at the camp. Some looked as though they thought it might be the last meal they ever ate, but not Dad. He calmly ate his porridge, finished his cup of tea, then stood up to address the apprehensive group.

'I can see fear on some of your faces. Don't be afraid. *God did not give us a spirit of fear but a spirit of power, love and self-control.* Finish your breakfast then take up your places as we discussed last night.'

I was halfway out to the kitchen with a pile of dirty plates when I heard the dull thud, thud, thud of helicopters in the distance. The sound grew louder until the helicopters were circling right over the campsite. It had begun.

'Mere, quick. Take these dishes out the back to Aunty's house.' Mum handed me a tray stacked high with crockery.

'That's the last of them, I think. Can you check that we've got everything out, just in case …' Her voice trailed off, not wanting to verbalise what awful possibilities lay ahead of us this morning.

68

'I have to be with your dad.'

She limped off to join the rest of the elders gathered on the porch of Te Arohanui, singing Maori songs and hymns.

'Hey Mum, can I come too?' My eldest son, Paul, ran to catch me up as I hurried back to the camp after dropping off the final tray of crockery. I spun around, almost twisting my ankle on the pot-holed road.

'No Paul, it's too dangerous for you kids. You know what your koro said: no kids allowed.'

'But I'm not a kid. I'm fourteen.'

'I said no, Paora.' Paora? Boy, I must be more uptight than I thought. I only used Paul's real name when I was mad at him. I deliberately softened my tone and gave him a cuddle.

'You're a good boy, Paul, and growing up fast. I know you want to be up there with the rest of us but I need you to help Aunty look after the younger children.'

A shout from a man stationed on the rickety wooden watchtower interrupted me. 'They're coming!' With a cigarette still burning between his fingers and binoculars pressed hard to his scarf-wrapped face the lookout pointed towards the city. There, like an endless trail of black huhu grubs marching along Tamaki Drive, were the army trucks and police rumbling towards Bastion Point. In the harbour stood an ominous grey navy ship, its guns trained directly at the camp. The helicopters swooped in low, whipping a wild wind around us. Paul clutched my arm. His voice wavered. 'What's going to happen? Will Nana and Koro be alright? Will you and Dad?'

Would we be all right? Who knew? I could see army trucks arriving at the bottom of the hill with bulldozers. Already hundreds of armed police were piling out and lining up in formation. I took a deep breath to calm my heart, which thumped as loud and fast as the helicopters hovering overhead.

'Go, my son. Run back to the house and stay there until Dad or I come and get you. Your koro has been praying all night. We will be fine.' I gave him a final hug, then a gentle push and watched him run down the road, almost tripping over the ruts in his haste to get to safety.

'Mere, I've been looking for you!' Doug rushed up and caught my arm, glancing at the rapidly retreating figure in the distance. 'Was that Paul?'

'He wanted to stay but I've sent him back to Arahia's.'

'Good. This is no place for kids. But come quickly, Mere. Stay near your mum. She might need you.'

'And I might need you.' My legs trembled . Was it fear, anger or sadness? I couldn't tell. Doug stopped for a moment and gathered me in his arms, kissing me on my forehead, my cheek, my lips.

'We will be fine, my love. Be strong. Now quick, we must be with the others when the police arrive.'

A few hundred people sat inside the wharenui. Young men flanked the building. Others were on the roof, standing staunch, proud and unarmed. I could feel the tension. On the porch, her arm wrapped firmly around a post and holding her flax kete, stood Mum. She had put on her white coat, the one she kept for special occasions, and she was, thankfully, wearing her knitted black and white hat. It was cold this morning. She jutted her chin out, proud and determined. It reminded me of my grandmother and the other kuia who had marched on parliament with Princess Te Puia so many years before. Would it always be like this? Defending the land against corrupt, greedy governments? Nothing had changed in over one hundred years. We offered the government land; they took it – and more. We defended our land; the government took more as a reprisal. We appealed through the law; they changed the laws. I looked around and saw cameras and journalists jotting notes. Perhaps this time would be different.

'Mum, are you okay?'

Staring straight ahead, her eyes focussed on the encroaching army of police, Mum enunciated each word through clenched cheeks. 'I will not leave this land. They will have to carry me off.'

I took up a position just behind her, sitting next to Aunty Joan. She was wrapped up warmly in a coat and scarf with a tartan rug over her knees, her sunken mouth singing 'Pa mai to reo aroha' – the song written especially to welcome the Maori soldiers home from World War Two. I had first heard it as a young child when her dad, Uncle Wiri and the others came home from the war – the war they had fought for this country, this government.

Two formal lines of police, uniformly dressed in dark blue coats and solid helmets, marched up the hill and surrounded the makeshift village, waiting for orders. There must have been at least seven or eight hundred of them.

'Haere mai, haere mai,' an elder called out. 'You are welcome to join us.'

An open-top jeep carrying two official looking men drove through a gap in the police encirclement. One man stood up with a microphone.

'That's the Commissioner of Crown Lands,' said Dad. 'Ignore him and keep singing. This is our land and we will remain on it, peacefully.'

The megaphone crackled as the Commissioner started his speech. 'I hereby officially inform every person who is not a member of the police or with the Department of Lands and Survey that he or she is a trespasser. I hereby require every such person to leave this place. I further warn that if such a person does not now leave this place, he or she will commit an offence under the Trespass Act 1968. Appropriate action will be taken against every person who fails to obey these warnings.'

The people kept singing. The cameras kept filming.

'This is Maori land,' called out one of the 'generals', his thick muscles tensing under his baggy black singlet.

'Yes it is, boy,' said an elder while continuing to stare defiantly at the officials. 'Keep your head. Maintain your dignity.'

'Ay, matua,' the 'general' replied, submitting to the older man's authority.

Now the Chief of Police took up the microphone. 'I again warn you that you are all wilful trespassers and a failure to leave at this time will render you liable to arrest. Whether you leave peacefully and with dignity or whether you are forcibly removed is a decision for you to make.'

The people kept singing. The cameras kept filming.

He motioned towards the hoards of police. They broke ranks and walked purposefully towards the protestors. Police buses reversed into position, ready to take the trespassers to jail.

'Ka mate, ka mate, ka ora, ka ora …' Some of the men broke into a haka, eyes wild and challenging. With the same vehemence that the men stamped their hands on their hips, I thrust my hands above my head. Yeah, let those dogs know what they were up against.

The swarm of blue uniforms moved closer, a few breaking off from the main group to arrest those closest to them.

The people kept singing. The cameras kept filming.

Two policemen marched directly towards Mum, still clutching the post with all her might. 'Come along, whaea,' one of them said. How did he know that word – the word of respect for an older Maori woman? I looked more closely at his brown skin and eyes half hidden under the police helmet. He was Maori!

'You bloody traitor! Have you no loyalty to your people?' I wanted to punch him in the face. 'How could you be on their side?'

The other policeman spoke up. He was Maori too. 'We're not on their side. We're just doing our job.'

'Then you should have quit your job,' I spat. 'You're a disgrace to our people.'

The two policemen ignored me and spoke again to Mum.

'Come along, whaea. We'll make sure you get safely to the van. Let us help you.'

The first policeman had tears in his eyes. Good job; let him suffer like we were.

Two policewomen came up to me.

'It is our duty to inform you that you are under arrest.' They gripped my arms and tried to walk me towards the vans. I planted my feet. They could carry me. There was no way I was taking one step off this land. With inscrutable faces, the two policewomen stepped off the porch, forcing me to step or trip. I dug my old shoes into the rough grass but the policewomen were strong. They kept walking with me hanging between them. All around me people were being firmly escorted away to the waiting buses. Some lay prostrate on the ground.

Two police were dragging one of the 'generals' by his arms, as he lay on his back. He looked as though he could easily overpower them with his massive biceps and thick, scarred knuckles but they hung limp in the heaving policemen's grip. He was making it as difficult as possible for them. Another young man was not so silent. He had wrapped his red scarf around his head like a bandana. At first glance it looked like his head was covered in blood. He wanted to fight. I could see the struggle in his eyes. He clenched his fists but used words instead.

'You bloody useless piece of –'

'Sir,' the policeman warned, 'I don't want to add verbal abuse of a police officer to your charges.' His thick leather gloves held the young man's arm in a vice-like grip.

'You call yourself a police officer? I thought police were meant to be on the good side.'

He kept walking, his eyes fixed on the buses, his progress impeded by the man's inert legs. Another police officer walked over to assist him. The man raised his voice, looking around him to make sure we all heard.

'Where's the justice here, ay?' He spat on the ground. Resolute police boots marched straight over it.

A photographer hurried closer to record the sight but a policeman stepped into his path. 'All media must leave now.' He pushed his palm straight into the camera lens, blocking the shot.

It was amazing that no one had thrown a punch. Plenty of these guys would bloody a nose for far less provocation than this. It was more than amazing; it was a miracle.

The policewomen pushed me into the bus. Those already on board started chanting the haka again. The door slammed. It started to bump across the grass joining a line of buses all filled with defiant, singing protestors. Our stand was not over yet.

'Filthy scabs.' I glared out the bus window back towards the village. Men were pulling corrugated iron sheets from the roofs and dismantling the buildings. The bulldozers which had been impatiently growling on the perimeter lumbered into the now desolate village, demolishing my home – yet again.

∾

73

16

HELENE

Helene adjusted the air conditioning in her car as she cruised north towards Noosa. The afternoon sun streamed through the autumn sky, heating the car to a summer degree. It was a beautiful day and even better, being a Friday. Russell had given her the day off. She had three days to enjoy Noosa's beaches and shops as well as attend the weekend conference. Three days away – from work, from home, from James. He was busier than ever, spending hours working to meet client deadlines. When he did finally arrive home he would flop in front of the television, exhausted. She had turned down two dinner invitations and as if that wasn't enough, her mother had turned up last Saturday morning on a bike. Helene was pruning the roses and almost dropped the shears in surprise as her mother, wearing psychedelic orange and blue cycle pants, rode up to the front gate.

'Mum! I didn't know you had taken up cycling.'

Her mother looked as excited as a child at Christmas. 'I thought you'd be surprised. I'm in training for my next trip to France.' She removed her bike helmet and combed her fingers through her flattened hair. 'Although goodness knows how anyone can look fashionably chic in one of these. Anyway, how are you darling? What have you been up to?'

'Just work as usual.' Helene snipped off a dead rose head.

'You really should take up some hobby or interest.'

'I do run and go to the gym, Mum.'

'Yes, of course, but something a little more exciting. I worry about you working all the time. There's more to life than work, you know. And James too. When are you going to have a holiday?'

'I'm off to Noosa soon.'

'Well that's a start. At least you two can relax on the beach and there are some lovely bush walks.'

'Actually I'm going on my own. It's a conference.'

'Oh.'

How was it that one word from her mother could carry such a multitude of meanings? Helene knew what 'Oh' meant: *A conference is not a holiday. You should be taking James. Too much time apart is not good for your marriage. I wish you could be less serious and have a little more fun.* It seemed that everyone's life was more exciting than hers. Nicolette was talking about sailing in the Whitsunday Islands on some rich bloke's boat and even Mel had spent all week raving to the nurses and patients about her weekend adventures at some rainforest retreat. It was all James' fault. He was so caught up with his work that he had no interest in doing anything else. It would be a relief to get away, even for a few days.

She stretched her legs as she reached the crest of Noosa Hill, anticipating the warm sand beneath her freshly painted toenails. Clear blue sea spread out before her. To her left, the Noosa River flowed into the sea, and beyond it golden beaches led the way north towards Fraser Island. To her right was Noosa's national park, with its sandy walking tracks meandering around the headland and descending into private, sandy coves perfect for swimming and snorkelling. She drove down the hill through lush native bush and into Noosa's famous Hastings Street. It ran parallel to the beach, separated only by the cafés, gourmet restaurants, elite fashion boutiques and luxury hotels that lined each side. Crowds of holiday makers, licking pastel coloured gelato, wandered past the 'latte set', relaxing at side-walk cafés with the newspaper, a glass of wine or an impeccably dressed child toying with his 'baby-cino'. Tanned, toned waiters adorned each café with casual efficiency. Equally tanned and toned women graced the boutiques, no doubt discussing the latest beauty therapy or investment strategy.

As Helene pulled up outside the hotel, a buxom, middle-aged woman encased in a tight white trouser suit sailed through the lobby doors. Gold and diamond jewellery glinted in the sun. She waved one bejewelled hand at the driver of a red convertible. He bounded out of the car with the energy of a man half his age and opened the door for her with a flourish and a kiss. It was such a glamorous, chivalrous scene, like something out of a 1950s movie. Watching them with a twinge of envy, Helene hoped it was a good omen for the weekend ahead.

After checking in, she changed into a short, floral skirt and headed for the shops. If you wanted great shoes you couldn't go past Hastings Street. After half an hour of trying everything from delicate pink Italian sandals to elegant brown boots she finally stepped out of the shop with a pair of extravagantly high stilettos complete with dainty gold beading. She felt like one of those advertisements for Italy, stepping out of the tiny shop into a cobblestone street swinging a large shopping bag, not a care in the world.

'Helene Mercer. What a surprise!' At the sound of that smooth, deep voice she spun around to face a man dressed in a white t-shirt, jeans and boots. She was momentarily speechless. Was this still her romantic daydream or was this real? She stared at him. He was certainly real, and vibrantly male. The five o'clock shadow, the toned pectorals and biceps, and the jeans that moulded around a definitely male physique. She gasped in recognition.

'Steve. Hi!' Was that all she could stammer out after all these years? She hadn't felt like this since medical school. He kissed her lightly on the cheek. She inhaled the familiar aftershave and managed to steady her voice, sounding far more composed than she felt.

'I can't believe it. What are you doing here in Noosa?'

He grinned. The crinkly smile lines around his eyes made her heart beat faster, just as it had that first time he'd spoken to her in the medical school cafeteria.

'I live here. Have done for about five years now.'

'Are you in general practice?'

'No way. I couldn't stand all that counselling and caring. I did plastic surgery. Went to the States for a while to learn a few tricks. Noosa is the place to be. Most of my patients escape the southern winter for a few weeks of sun, relaxation and a little body enhancement. They head home with a better tan, fewer wrinkles and their friends are none the wiser!'

'It sounds the ideal job, surrounded by sun, sea and beautiful women.'

'More beautiful when I've finished with them.' He glanced towards a passing blonde, his eyes scanning the voluptuous curves beneath her red sundress. Then his gaze was back on her.

'So Helene, what are you up to now? Saving the world? Volunteering your services to Medicine Sans Frontiers on some remote African mission?'

'Nothing like that. I work in Brisbane at a general practice in the city.'

'Helene Mercer: Mercer by name, mercy by nature. Isn't that what we used to joke about? Where did all your good intentions go?'

'Oh, you know. We all have these idealistic plans when we're young but life gets in the way.' She brushed it off lightly, bottling the disquiet brewing in her mind. It was true: she had dreamed of doing something adventurous and noble like her granddad, something that would make a difference. What had happened? *You got married, that's what happened.* Another of those unbidden thoughts assaulted her mind. She absently rubbed her ring finger – no ring, just eczema. Despite removing her wedding rings and slathering on hydrocortisone cream, it refused to heal.

Steve ran both hands through his short cropped hair, his biceps bulging out from under the t-shirt. 'Life …yeah. It throws itself at you. I just throw myself back at it.' He looked at her left hand. 'What about you? I see you haven't thrown yourself across the marriage altar yet.'

'Actually I have. A few years ago.'

'Is he up here with you?'

'No. I'm here for work. Well, as much work as you do at these weekend conferences.'

'Great. So you'll have plenty of time to spend with me.' Steve wrapped an arm around her shoulders. 'Hey, I'm free tonight. If you have no plans how about we catch up on old times?'

A few hours later Helene was sipping wine at a candlelit table overlooking the beach. It was the sort of situation Nicolette would adore: a spontaneous, grabbing of the moment and recklessly plunging into whatever the evening held in store. Her excitement quashed a few niggling guilt pangs. She was allowed to enjoy herself. She deserved it.

'Helene, you look fantastic, as always.' Steve smiled and raised his glass. His charm had not dwindled a bit. He could still make the plainest woman feel like a supermodel. She did feel good, though. When was the last time she had spent so much time on her make-up? It was like university days all over again.

'Thanks. You look pretty good yourself.' That was the understatement of the year. She raised her glass to Steve's. 'Here's to chance encounters.'

'Chance encounters.' Steve grinned. 'I like the sound of that.'

Helene took a sip of wine, then another more generous mouthful. 'Have you eaten here before?'

'It's my local. The chef's a mate of mine – great food – but it's the setting that really makes it. How many places in the world can you dine outside, right on the beach, in the middle of winter?'

They weren't exactly outside; the waiters had pulled huge doors across to protect diners from the cool beach breeze, but who cared about details?

'I don't know why I don't come up here more often. It's so close to Brisbane. I guess I just get caught up with work and the daily grind. Do you ever get down there?'

Steve relaxed back in his seat, legs casually crossed, his long fingers toying with the wine glass. 'Business takes me to Brisbane occasionally. But it's the big cities I miss: Rome, Paris, Bangkok.'

'I adore Thailand.' A memory of her and James laughing in a tiny Bangkok food stall, car fumes and dust swirling off the street, sweat pouring off their foreheads as they ate green curry flashed through her mind.

'But you can't go past a pastis on a hot summer's evening in Paris. There's nothing better."

'Really? Not even the Parisian women?'

Steve laughed. 'Perhaps.' His eyes twinkled at her in that old, familiar way.

'My mother is the quintessential Francophile.' Helene sipped her wine. 'She lectures in French at the university and is always zipping over to France. You and she would have lots to talk about.'

'I'm sure we would.' He leaned over to refill her glass then looked at her in the same way her sister looked at chocolate. 'But right now I'm far more interested in you.'

She felt that familiar fluttering in her chest and a velvet wave washed through her as she returned Steve's hungry gaze. This was just as she had imagined when she had put the thought out to the universe at the café. About to take another sip of wine, she stopped abruptly, almost spilling the generously filled glass. It couldn't just be coincidence, could it, that she had imagined herself with Steve and here he was?

'Hey Helene, what's up? You look as though you've seen a ghost.'

She smothered her disquiet with a smile. 'It's nothing. Everything's perfect.' She glanced at a neighbouring table. 'The food looks wonderful. Shall we order?'

The entree arrived as they started on their second bottle of pinot gris. Steve's drinking tastes had clearly matured since their beer-swilling medical school days. Half a bottle later, Helene asked the question that had been burning in her mind.

'So are there any women in your life? I can't imagine you without at least a few around.'

'No one special at the moment. I gave the marriage thing a go for a couple of years but it didn't work out.'

'What happened?'

'We were in the States. I was studying. She got tired of me always being at the hospital or the library. So she found some rich Yank and I came home alone.'

He had that little lost boy look that always made her want to wrap him in her arms. 'How awful.'

'It worked out okay. By the time we split up we felt pretty much nothing for each other. Actually it was a relief not to have her nagging me all the time.'

Steve slipped his hand under the table and lightly brushed it along Helene's thigh. 'But that's history and now I have plenty of time, all night if you like.'

That fleeting touch sent a velvet wave surging through her body. This was getting dangerous. She was a married woman. Another thought countered. *Lots of women do this. It may even be good for your marriage – a boost of self-esteem and a bit of competition to snap James into action.*

She reached for her glass of wine. Steve's hand wrapped around hers on the glass, his fingers entwining hers. His eyes burned. 'After all these years I'd forgotten how kissable you are. How did I ever let you go? I must have been crazy.'

He wasn't the one who had been crazy; it was her. She had been crazy to go out with him as long as she did. None of the other registrars seemed to work quite as many night shifts and weekends. She had tried to brush off the rumours about him and that nurse. She was drawn by his magnetic appeal, leaving all remnants of reason and sensibility lying inert in a firmly shut recess of her mind.

'Yes, you were.'

Steve laughed, raised his glass to hers and drained it. 'Well I'm not crazy now. Shall we go?'

The restaurant spilled out onto a boardwalk that ran the length of the beach. It was chilly outside and Steve placed his arm around Helene's waist, holding her close as they walked. The bright lights and din of the restaurant faded to waves breaking on the dark, almost deserted beach. Steve guided Helene to a bench seat tucked into the embrace of an enormous pandanus palm. He drew her down onto the seat and stroked her cheek. His closeness, his aftershave, the waves, the beach, the wine – her senses reeled. He leaned closer to brush his lips against hers. Her body pulsed. Her lips melted into his.

'Sleep with me.' His voice was smooth and dark like rich, forbidden chocolate. She could hardly breathe. She didn't want to. He kissed her again, forcefully, passionately. She pressed closer to his body and drank it in. Minutes passed, or was it hours, before he pulled away and murmured in her ear. 'Let's go to your room.'

They floated towards the hotel through the late night diners and party-goers.

'Good evening, Doctor Mercer.'

She could almost hear the chocolate bubble burst. She forced a smile. It was Lloyd, one of her patients. His sunburnt, hairy arm was draped over a petite, blond woman's shoulders. She staggered like an over-ambitious weight-lifter.

'This is my wife, Judy. We're up here for a golfing weekend. What about you?' He grinned at Steve. 'A romantic weekend away with your husband, I bet.' He grabbed Steve's hand, shaking it vigorously. 'So you've managed to whisk Helene away from her patients. I keep her busy seeing all my executives – a big job. I think there's a few lined up for next week. No rest for the wicked, eh?'

He winked at the two of them. Had he guessed the truth? Helene's heart beat and her face flushed, desire replaced by embarrassment.

Steve didn't seem at all fazed. He steered the niceties to a quick end and, with his arm still firmly around her, guided her towards the hotel. 'That was fun, playing your husband. How long have we been married?'

Helene's head began to throb. This was not the delicious throbbing of earlier in the evening. This was painful and oppressive. She tried to ignore it but it pressed relentlessly into her temples, crushing her desire and blurring her vision. Her stomach churned. Just as they reached the hotel lobby she stopped, clutching her stomach. 'I think I'm going to be sick.'

Frustration flickered across Steve's face. 'Let's get you to your room. You'll feel okay soon.'

She leaned against the wall, steadying herself against the black pounding in her head. 'No, I don't think this will go away.' She clenched her teeth and hoped she wouldn't spew on the polished tiles. How embarrassing would that be? 'I think I just need to get to bed. I'm so sorry. Call me tomorrow. I'm in room 216.'

She stumbled to her room and fumbled in her bag for the room card. The nausea and headache weren't so bad now. She let herself in. She could see perfectly well again. Her eyes swept across the bed to the phone. No red light flashing for messages. James hadn't called. That didn't seem like him; he always phoned. Oh well, she would be back home on Sunday. She collapsed into the luxurious king sized bed, closed her eyes and fell asleep alone.

17

JAMES

James stretched out on the leather settee, twisted the top off his stubby of beer and flicked the remote at the screen. The channel switched from news to sports. Two commentators, one an ex-Blues player who looked as though he'd rather be in his rugby gear than the stiff navy suit and checked tie, were doing the lead-up to the big game. The house seemed empty without Helene and yet in some ways it was a relief that she was away for the weekend. He would be able to chill out in front of the rugby all evening without the usual pall of guilt. It was weird; she came from a family of virtual sportaholics – they both did – but she hated the one sport he most loved. She refused to go to a game or even watch it on television. At least his mum pretended to enjoy it. But the way Helene sighed as she tidied the kitchen or when she gathered up her medical textbooks and marched off to the bedroom put a dampener on the whole evening.

It hadn't always been like this. When they first met one Sunday afternoon at Southbank she was watching a small group of formally dressed musicians seated on fold-out chairs in a secluded grassy area. A handful of picnickers sprawled on tartan rugs in front of them, Bach and Beethoven swirling around their strawberries and plastic champagne flutes. She was standing apart from the crowd, sipping her water bottle, her eyes, along with the rest of the band, on the woman playing a violin solo. But it was what she wore that grabbed James' attention. Draped over one shoulder, partially covering her exposed, tanned stomach and tight white shorts was a coil of rope.

Her hair was pulled up into a dark pony tail and she stood like a glistening Amazon woman … well perhaps a more clover honey, Australian version. He had been determined to talk to her.

'They're pretty good, aren't they?' He nodded towards the band. She had turned and smiled at him.

'I'm not really a connoisseur of classical music. I just came to listen to my mum. It's her first time playing a concerto in public. She's a bit nervous.'

James tapped his foot against the heavy rope she had dumped onto the grass.

'So how does the rope fit in? Is it the latest fashion accessory for classical music lovers?'

She grinned. 'Of course! Haven't you heard of the 'Absailing Arias? We play Chopin while we climb.' She nodded towards Kangaroo Point – a popular place for rock climbers.

'You're kidding, right?'

She laughed, melting and heating his insides all at once.

'About the arias, yes. About the rock climbing, no. My friends and I climb every weekend. It's fun.'

Fun. They'd had a lot of fun in those early days. He had joined her rock-climbing buddies and spent most weekends hiking through rainforest or over parched farmland in search of the perfect cliff to conquer. After they were married they went off more on their own, just the two of them, cycling, skiing, diving. It was only in the past year, since setting up the business, that things had changed. Now the nearest he got to an adrenaline rush was dodging the kamikaze magpies nesting in the gum trees on his early morning runs. But you couldn't pay a mortgage or establish a business by taking off on expensive sporting pursuits all the time. He just wished Helene felt the same.

He ripped open a large bag of potato crisps, dug in to grab a handful and dropped the crackling bag on the coffee table, right next to his feet. Beer and chips – what more could a bloke want? Maybe his wife next to him. Too bad he couldn't make her like rugby any more than she could make him like some of her scatty friends. He returned his attention to the game and assessed the line-up. The Aussies weighed in slightly heavier than the Kiwis but you could never under-estimate those All Blacks. It took more than brute power to win at this level. Mind you the Aussies, with their new coach and fresh back from training camp, looked in good shape. It could go either way.

The front door bell rang. Who would call around on a Friday night, just when the rugby was about to start? John was away for the weekend and most of the other guys were in town watching the game at the pub. James decided to ignore it in the hope they'd go away. He took another handful of chips and a swig of beer. The players lined up on the field, facing each other, ready to sing their national anthems. The insistent ringing of the door bell echoed along the hall's polished floor and bounced through the empty house, demanding to be heard. Still holding his beer, James flicked the television to mute and reluctantly headed for the door.

'Hi, James. My television's packed up. I was stuck all alone at home and wondered who else would be watching the game tonight and I thought of you! I knew you'd like some company.' Nicolette stood at the door, a six pack clasped under her breasts, making them almost spill out of her clingy red singlet. 'I brought a few beers,' she passed them to him, and reached into the shopping bag swinging by her side, 'and some prawns. Nothing like fresh prawns to go with a cold beer.'

'I guess not.' James tried to sound enthusiastic.

'Beer and prawns. It's to us Aussies what wine and cheese is to the French.' She laughed at her own joke and, twisting her arm behind her, jabbed her keys at her red convertible parked on the street. Its lights blinked on and off. She touched his arm. Boy, those nails could really do some damage.

'So shall we stand out here all night or are you going to invite me in?'

'Sure, Nicolette. Come in.' James held the door open and watched her stilettos click down the hallway, leaving tiny pock-marks on the polished wood. He put the pack of beer in the fridge, pulling one out for his guest, and returned to the lounge where she was already curled up on the settee, her stilettos abandoned under the coffee table. He sat in the chair, careful to keep his distance. She was Helene's friend, not his. He didn't want to appear rude but it somehow felt wrong that she was here, with him, dressed like that.

'Look at number eight run!' She was already engrossed in the game, oblivious to his discomfort. Perhaps he was overreacting. They both liked rugby. Why not enjoy the game together? He had always thought she preferred the players to the actual game but apparently not. He tilted his head back and let the bitter-sweet liquid trickle down his throat. The Aussie team was on fire tonight, especially that number eight. Nicolette was right.

The Kiwis had the ball now.

'Tackle him. Get in there!' Nicolette sprang forward, transfixed to the screen.

'Yes!' She punched the air triumphantly. A brick-solid back flew at the runner's legs, knocking him to the ground.

'They're in good shape. Better than last season. Must be that training camp. I heard it was tough this year with the new coach.' She pulled out her hair clip letting her blond hair cascade over her shoulders.

'Yeah, I think we're in with a chance,' James agreed.

'What are you thinking, ref?' Nicolette was yelling at the screen again. The referee was holding up a yellow card and signalling for the Aussie captain to come over.

'That tackle was fine. Nothing wrong with it!'

At half-time James got up to throw out the discarded prawn shells and fetch more beer. The last two bottles. They had powered through a fair few; Nicolette could knock them back as well as any bloke.

'We've run out of beer. Sorry.' He passed the final brown stubby to her. Her fingers brushed his as she took the bottle - cool and inviting.

'No problem. I always come prepared.' She knelt up on the

settee and leaned over the back for her bag. A thin band of white lace stretched above her jeans, curving across her bare back. His heart beat faster. She heaved the bag onto the floor in front of her. What did women keep in those things?

She pulled out a bottle of vodka and a large bottle of diet tonic. 'Sorry, the tonic's not chilled. Do you have any ice?'

'Sure but I'm not really into vodka.' He wished he had more beer.

'Just have a small one. I'm sure you'll like it.' She showed him the bottle. 'It's mango. Once you've had one you'll want more.'

That was what he was worried about. Beer and spirits weren't a good mix, especially the night before an eighty kilometre cycle. 'Okay, just a small one.'

The second half started just as he returned with the ice bucket. The Kiwis had come out strong and scored two tries in the first five minutes. It didn't look good. James knocked back the vodka as though it was beer. Nicolette quietly refilled the glass: half vodka, half ice with a splash of tonic.

'You're right. It's pretty good.' James leaned over from his chair to take the glass from Nicolette. She held it just out of his reach.

'Come over here and get it.' She patted the space on the settee next to her. 'Then you can help yourself and stop distracting me from the game.'

That made sense. He moved over to the settee. Nicolette was back into the game. It wasn't going well.

'What's wrong with our team? They're letting those Kiwis walk all over them. Where's the backup? Did you see that?' She turned towards James so vehemently that her drink sloshed onto his shirt.

'Oh, sorry.' She touched the wet shirt, her fingers spreading across his chest, pressing, sliding up over his shoulder and down his arm.

'Mm, nice biceps. I like a man with strong arms.' Her fingers were cool against the heat of his arm. He slugged back the last of his drink, noticing how strands of her blonde hair brushed across her chest, getting caught in the deep cleavage that plunged below her red top. Imagine being a strand of that hair …

'Yes! Yes!' She released his arm and was leaning forward, elbows on knees, her red top straining to hold in its bouncing contents. He dragged his eyes back to the screen and tried to focus.

'Go! Go!' she screamed.

An Aussie forward had the ball and was sprinting for the try line. The clock showed three minutes until fulltime. They could still win the game. The forward dove over the try line, slamming the ball on the ground just before he disappeared under a pile of pursuers. Try! The score was twenty to nineteen. James poured the last of the vodka into their glasses.

'We just need the conversion to win. I reckon we'll do it.'

'I'm sure we will. Come on, boys. You can do it.'

They sat together on the edge of the settee, holding their vodka and their breath as the ball flew in an arc over the field – and over the goalpost.

'Yes!' James raised his glass to Nicolette's and then sculled the vodka in one shot. She did the same and they smashed their glasses down on the table. It felt like university days all over again. Nicolette was laughing as she flung her arms around James' neck.

'What a game! I thought it was all over and then look how they came back! It was fantastic!' She kissed the back of his neck, trailing her lips, her teeth, her tongue towards his ear.

'Let's celebrate.' Her words purred like a well-oiled engine.

He gripped the edge of the settee, fighting for control. Her lips found his and he drank in pure, sweet honey. 'No, Nicolette. We can't do this.'

She pressed herself against him. He lost his balance, falling back along the settee with Nicolette on top.

'We can't do what? Do you mean this?' She lowered herself slowly, seductively towards him, the red top filling his vision. So this was how it felt to be a strand of her hair. He breathed in sweet musk and moaned. She knelt above him and, button by button, undid the red top. He could not tear his eyes away.

'You know you want me,' she purred. 'And I want you. I've wanted you for a long time.' She had a tiny red rose tattooed where he shouldn't be looking, where he couldn't stop looking. 'Let's enjoy ourselves this one night. Helene need never know. It can be our little secret.' She kissed him again. The room went dark, the television silent. He sank into an intoxicating haze of blond hair, red roses and sweet musk.

A noise shattered the haze, a persistent, banging noise. Someone was knocking at the front door. His head cleared. He pushed Nicolette off him and stood up, running his hands through his tousled hair and straightening his damp shirt.

'Don't answer it. Stay here with me.' Nicolette reached up to kiss him again.

He pushed her away. 'I think you'd better go.' He stumbled down the hallway in the dark. Strange, he didn't remember switching off the lights. Someone was definitely at the front door. It looked like another woman. Just what he needed.

'Hello, James. I'm so sorry to bother you at this time of night but I don't have a torch or candles.' It was Mere.

'A torch? Candles?' James was lost.

'Yes. I wondered if I could borrow a candle. I think the whole street has lost its power.'

James looked up the street. It was dark apart from the flash of Nicolette's car unlocking as she tiptoed down the side of the house, blew him a kiss and drove away.

18

Helene woke up early Saturday morning, pulled on her running gear and headed for Noosa National Park. The barely risen sun was already burning away the overnight chill. Kookaburras cackled high up in the rainforest. Rosellas darted through the trees, their brilliant green, red and yellow plumage like neon signs against the grey-green gums. She dodged a lizard scurrying towards the safety of a rock. Crisp air hit her moist skin. Invigorated, she bounded along the track, barely noticing the steep parts. The wine last night hadn't seemed to affect her, apart from the sudden headache. It had disappeared as quickly as it had come, lasting only long enough to sabotage her night with Steve. Sabotage or save? Perhaps it was a blessing in disguise. What was she thinking? Jumping into bed with an old flame as soon as she met him? Steve, of all people. Yet she hadn't felt this alive since James had wheeled his bike into her life that day at Southbank. If only they could recapture those feelings ... but it was impossible. Everyone knew that once the feelings were gone there was little hope.

Below the track, through banksias and pandanus palms, waves lapped the shore of a secluded bay. Steam vapours rose off the rocks. A lone swimmer, sleek and black, powered through the water. She kept running, replaying the events of the previous evening. They'd had so much to talk about, so much to catch up on, and when Steve had confided how his wife had left him, that little lost school boy look had made him seem so vulnerable. Perhaps he had changed, become more sensitive, more loyal? One thing certainly hadn't changed; he was as dangerously attractive as ever. That kiss ... her heart raced. She stopped at a lookout area perched high above wave battered rocks to catch her breath, inhaling the wild sea and eucalyptus scented air.

Back at the hotel, she checked her mobile and hotel phone. Still nothing from James. She dialled home and left a message. 'Hi, James. I guess you're still out cycling. Hope you had a good night. I'm just off to the conference. I'll try to call later. Bye.'

There was a sharp rap at the door. 'Flowers for Dr Collins.' The porter handed her a huge bouquet of red roses. Breathing in the fragrance she closed the door and excitedly searched for a card. Boldly scrawled in black it read: *Dreamt of you last night xxx S.*

Later that morning Helene sat in the dimmed lecture room trying to keep her eyes open. Lack of sleep and too much alcohol were finally catching up with her. Even the enthusiasm of the cardiologist as he flicked through graphic slides of diseased arteries interspersed with gondolas and pyramids from recently attended conferences couldn't hold her attention. Steve had dreamt about her last night. Would he call? She hadn't even thought to get his number. What if he did? Should she see him again? All these years later and he could still stir feelings in her that she was sure had died. He was impossibly unfaithful – 'brains in his pants'. That's what her friends had consoled her with after their breakup. 'Find someone more stable.' She had.

The audience clapped. Helene joined in, thanking the cardiologist for whatever he had taught them. Helene switched on her mobile phone – two messages. She walked past the trade displays and buffet tables laden with fresh fruit and healthy looking filled rolls out to the pool area and pressed 'Listen' on her phone.

'Hey, babe.' Only Steve had ever called her that. 'Can't stop thinking about last night. Shame about your headache. Dying to see you but I'm tied up all weekend. I'm coming to Brisbane soon. I'll text you. Love ya.'

She felt warm all over and it wasn't just the midday sun. This was like some soap opera; a married woman lounging by a five-star pool taking illicit calls from an old lover. Surely there was nothing wrong with seeing him again. They could just chat, couldn't they?

19

JAMES

James stared out his office window. It was bucketing down. Rain squalled in heavy sheets across the street. A car crept down the road, its driver peering through the windscreen for a spare park. His abandoned computer had reverted to screen saver: a photo of him and Helene with heavy back packs and wide grins, posing at the edge of an escarpment high above lush rainforest. He'd been on a roll this morning, churning out some great designs for his client's brochure – until the text message. Now he was staring past snail-paced cars and sodden, scurrying people, his mind far from work.

He had hardly seen Helene since her weekend in Noosa. Pending work deadlines had consumed his weekend. When he finally walked in the door on Sunday evening she had hardly even kissed him. Dinner had been ham and cheese toasted sandwiches in front of television. The Sunday documentary filled in the silent gaps between them. Did she suspect that Nicolette had been over? Perhaps he should have told her straight up. Better than her finding out some other way. But how would she find out and what would he say anyway? That her friend had tried to seduce him? His mum always said 'there's no smoke without fire' whenever she and her Country Women's Association friends gossiped over their weekly cups of tea and pumpkin scones. Would Helene believe that he hadn't encouraged Nicolette? Would she believe that nothing had happened between them? It was better to pretend it had never happened. Surely Nicolette had got the message and would move onto some other bloke. He wouldn't even tell John. He knew what he would say: 'You're bloody mad, mate. A hot sheila throws herself at you and you say no. Tell her to come and see me. I'll show her a good time.'

A good time was all very well and he had almost succumbed – he wasn't made of stone. If Mere hadn't knocked on the door asking for a candle he would have a lot more to hide from Helene. He picked up his mobile and read the message again.

'Have a business proposition. Call me.'

The message itself wasn't what threw him. It was the graphic at the end of the message – a red rose. No wonder he couldn't concentrate on his work. He pressed delete.

'Sorry, James. I'll just be a moment,' his receptionist called out from the front room. She scraped her chair back from her desk and hurried out the door that led to the bathroom. Her morning sickness was as bad as ever. It might be two minutes or twenty before she returned looking as though she had just run around the block. He turned back to his computer screen and reopened the file on his latest account. This one would pay for the month's expenses with enough to tide him over until Bob's contract came through. He couldn't afford to waste time staring out windows or worrying about text messages.

The door opened. For a split second he thought it was his receptionist returning in record time but it was the other door that now clicked shut. Someone had come in off the street and by the sounds of those shoes it was a woman. He walked out to see who it was.

'Darling, thank goodness you're here! I was just down the road at a photo shoot when the rain hit. The film crew have all taken refuge at a café round the corner. The actor's hair's a mess and the cameraman is refusing to film in the wet.' Nicolette set two take-out coffees on the receptionist's desk and her dripping umbrella in a corner. 'Did you get my text?'

James couldn't help noticing how her wet clothes melded around her body like she was in a wet t-shirt competition. 'I just read it. Haven't had a chance to reply.'

'Never mind. I'm here now. It's better if we talk face to face, and being just around the corner, I thought, why not grab the bull by the horns, so to speak?' She peeled off her sodden jacket and hung it on the antique coat stand. 'It's freezing out there.' She wrapped her arms around herself.

'Come through to my office. The heater's on.'

She padded in after him, stilettos in hand.

'That rain is merciless. Mind if I put these by the heater?' She positioned the shoes in front of the heater then plonked into the visitor's chair.

How long was she planning to stay? He had work to do.

'Oh, the coffee – can't let it get cold. There's nothing worse than cold coffee.' She jumped up, disappeared into the front room and returned, handing him the still hot coffee.

'Thanks.'

'So would you like to hear my proposition?' She sat back in the chair, legs crossed demurely, as though this was an important business meeting, despite her bare feet.

'Sure.' He didn't know what else to say.

'Well ...' Nicolette paused as though she was about to tell him that she'd won lotto. 'I don't know why I didn't think of this sooner. It only occurred to me when the advertising agency we usually use shut down last week. Actually, they didn't shut down; they were amalgamated into another agency which means most of the people we deal with have been fired.'

James slugged back his coffee. A caffeine hit was just what he needed. 'That's bad news. These mega corporations are pretty ruthless about things like that.'

'Exactly. That's why we're not so keen to automatically give the new guys our business. We were discussing it yesterday and I suddenly thought of you. You do exactly what they did for us, don't you?'

This sounded promising. 'I design brochures, websites, that sort of thing. Is that what you need?'

Nicolette smiled at him. It reminded him of his brother's smile when they played chess. He always won. No, it wasn't like that. Nicolette was simply offering him some work, and loads of it, by the sounds.

'Do you have anything I can look at now? What are you working on at the moment?'

He'd been dying to show someone this latest logo. That was one thing he missed from his old job. 'It's still confidential but I guess there's no harm in you seeing it.'

Nicolette walked around to his side of the desk and leaned over his shoulder. He could smell her perfume and feel her coffee mint breath brushing past his cheek. If he moved, he would touch her. He clicked open the 'Silver Service' file. Up came an image of two silver stylised S shapes moulded together with ornate flourishes, 'This is the logo I've almost finished. It's going on their new range of gourmet pet food.'

'Wow! It's fantastic. Did you design that?'

'Sure. Now I'm working on the layout for their point-of-sale and print advertisements.' He flicked to another page. 'And this is a website layout I did for a company last week.' She was so close. The tension was like a taut wire.

'We could sure do with a talent like yours on our team. It's just what we need.' She walked back around to her chair. 'I love your work and I'm sure my boss will too. Would you be able to e-mail me those layouts and that logo to show her? If she likes your style we can set up a meeting to discuss details.'

'How about I send a couple of others? I can't send that logo before I give it to my client.'

Nicolette put her hand to her forehead as though she had a headache. Then she looked up with tears in her eyes. Where had this come from?

'I'm sorry, James. I'm sorry about everything. The other night … I don't know what I was thinking. I was just so upset. Brad dumped me last week and I couldn't bear to spend the weekend on my own.' She sniffed delicately. 'And now my boss is on my case to find a new designer this week. She has such high expectations. I can't just hire the first person I come across. He has to be the best to keep her happy.

What you've just shown me is sure to convince her you're the man for the job. If you send me something else, I just don't know …'

She dabbed at her tears, and then looked up at him with puppy dog eyes. He wanted to help her and he wanted the work, but there was no way he could give her those designs; it wasn't ethical. The phone started ringing in the front room. His receptionist was still in the bathroom. 'Hold on a moment. I need to grab that call.' He strode into the other room and answered the phone – a supplier confirming his address. He hurried back. Nicolette was by his computer. 'I'm just having one last look at these designs. You have a real talent, you know.'

'Glad you like it.'

She picked up her bag from his desk and smiled at him. 'Oh, I do.'

She walked over to the heater and slid into her stilettos. 'I'll look forward to seeing whatever you can send me. I think your style will really fit well with ours.'

James walked her to the door. The rain had stopped. She picked up her umbrella and jacket and turned towards him. 'I hope Helene knows how lucky she is to have you.'

Before he could stop himself his mounting doubts spilt out. 'I'm not sure about that.'

She pecked him on the cheek and whispered, 'If you were mine I'd make sure you knew.' Her finger trailed down his chest, his stomach; he held his breath. Then with a sultry smirk she spun on her high heels, leaving him in a haze of perfume. He took a deep breath to calm himself.

'Are you going out?' He glanced around to see his receptionist coming back from the bathroom.

'Do you have to sneak in so quietly? You made me jump.'

She laughed and plonked down at the desk. 'I didn't mean to scare you.' She looked more closely at him. 'What's wrong? You look a bit tense.'

'It's nothing. I'm fine. Probably had too much coffee, that's all.' Then changing the subject, 'Are you okay now?'

She tapped her keyboard and smiled up at him. 'Right as rain – at least for another hour.'

He headed back to his desk determined to finish the 'Silver Service' project before the end of the day.

It was six-thirty that evening when his mobile rang. The receptionist had gone home hours ago after a prolonged vomiting session. It was Helene.

'Where are you? I thought you said you'd be home early tonight?' She sounded like his mother.

'I'm almost finished. Probably another hour will do it.'

'Another hour! You said you'd cook tonight.'

He banged his hand against his forehead. He'd completely forgotten. 'Sorry, I'll pick up some takeaways on the way home. Do you want pizza or Thai?'

'I can't wait that long. I'll get something myself.'

20

HELENE

Helene dumped the phone on its stand and pulled out a can of baked beans. Dinner for one, yet again. James had been late every night this week. They had hardly seen each other since she'd come home from the weekend in Noosa. It seemed like weeks rather than days ago. Was this how her mum had felt all those years ago? She remembered the arguments late at night when she should have been safely asleep. She would tiptoe out of her bedroom and peek around the corner of the lounge to see her father sprawled on the couch nursing the whiskey bottle. Her mother stood in front of him, her face mottled with emotion, twisting her rings like churning butter.

'You promised you would be home for dinner tonight. Couldn't you once, just once, keep your promise?'

The smell of oven dried-out dinner soured the air but her Mum smelt something else. 'And don't tell me your 'business deal' didn't involve some woman with bad taste in perfume.'

Her father smiled his scary smile; the one that could at any moment switch to a vicious snarl. He pushed himself out of his seat and stumbled over to her mum, wrapping his arms around her waist and kissing her neck with slobbery kisses.

'Ah, me love. But you're the one I love.'

She pushed him away, wiping the spittle from her neck. 'If you loved us, you wouldn't waste all the money on women and grog.'

His scary smile switched. Helene would turn and run back to her bedroom, their snarling snapping at her heels like wild dogs.

She tipped the baked beans into a pot and banged it on the gas stove. Where was the man she had married: the adventurer, the romantic, the one who wasn't like her father? This wasn't how it was meant to be. The baked beans bubbled. Bright orange spits splattered her cream suit. Great. She poured the sloppy mess onto a plate, grabbed a fork and sat down at the kitchen table. She was about to take a mouthful when her mobile rang.

'Hey, Helene.'

The voice swept baked beans off the menu and replaced it with smooth, dark chocolate.

'Steve! I didn't expect to hear from you so soon.' Helene jumped up from the table and walked out to the lounge, escaping the banal beans in their beastly orange sauce.

'Soon? It's been at least four days and I can't get you out of my mind. I'm coming down to Brisbane tomorrow. How about we catch up for a drink after work, around six?'

'I'd love to. Where?'

'The Pavilion Bar at the Stamford Plaza. I'm staying there. And babe, have you still got those stockings?'

Helene flushed. She knew exactly which stockings he was thinking of.

'Why?'

'Wear them for old time's sake. Ciao.'

Suddenly she didn't feel hungry. She scrolled through her iPod, selected a couple of favourite tracks from med school days, poured herself a glass of wine and dumped the congealed baked beans in the bin. It was time to call Nicolette.

'Hi, Nic, it's me, Helene.'

'Helene, darling. How was your weekend? I've been dying to find out.'

Helene settled into the lounge chair and took a sip of wine. 'You'll never believe it! I tried that universe thing you suggested and it worked.'

'See, I told you it works. What happened?'

'Do you remember I told you about Steve, my boyfriend from med school?'

'Wasn't he the one you caught with that nurse?'

'That was years ago. I don't think he's like that now.' Helene brushed the question off like an annoying mosquito. 'Anyway, that doesn't matter. I bumped into him in Noosa and we had dinner together. It was amazing.'

'The dinner or meeting him?'

'Both!' She sipped more wine, relishing the languorous glow radiating through her body.

'I hope you didn't do anything I wouldn't.'

'Of course not – I'm a married woman. But as you said, I needed some excitement and I got it. And guess what? He's in town tomorrow night. I'm meeting him for a drink after work.'

'Just a drink, I hope.'

Helene giggled. 'Of course just a drink. I probably won't be home much later than James. He hasn't been home before eight all week. We've hardly seen each other.'

'Ships in the night.'

'You could say that.'

'And you're sure that your ship will be dutifully docked at home by eight pm?'

Helene hesitated. What did she really expect to happen tomorrow night?

Nicolette laughed. 'Don't worry, darling. I won't tell. Go ahead and enjoy what the universe has brought to you.'

'Thanks, Nic.'

'What are friends for?'

Helene snapped her phone shut. Something didn't feel quite right. She wandered into the bedroom to find a pile of neatly folded clothes at the end of the bed. Since Mere had arrived she hadn't had to do any washing or ironing. Each day she arrived home to find the washing done and the floors mopped. It was wonderful. She kept meaning to invite Mere over for dinner, although most nights the guest house was dark by nine. She looked out the window. Only the bedroom light was on. Through the sheer curtain she saw Mere's silhouette kneeling beside the bed with arms outstretched above her. Then she lowered her arms and bowed her head, her face awash with peace.

21

It was after five the next afternoon when Helene finally found a moment to fix her stockings. Her toe had been poking through a hole in the lace, irritating her as much as the incessant excuses she had fielded all day. Lloyd had been true to his word and sent his entire senior management team in. It had taken up most of the day. This corporate work paid well which kept Russell generous with the salaries he paid his doctors. But today, for the first time since she had started this job, she felt different. Was she really having any impact on these work-obsessed men? Even when presented with alarming cholesterol or blood pressure results, most seemed in denial. If she suggested they quit smoking: 'I've tried before but it helps calm my nerves. I'll give it another go once this deal is brokered.' If she suggested eating more fruit and vegetables: 'My wife is always nagging me to eat more of that rabbit food. Just give me the drugs, doc. They'll do the job, won't they?' They seemed to think they were invincible, that their body could handle the constant abuse and still keep going. If Lloyd hadn't forced them to come in they would blithely continue until a heart attack or worse.

Helene rested her foot on the desk and dabbed clear nail varnish around the edge of the torn lace. That would seal it at least for tonight. Thank goodness for Mel, the nail polish queen. The reception desk displayed as many nail polish bottles as pens. The colours changed as frequently as Mel's boyfriends. Today was black, in honour of the greasy looking bloke with the skull t-shirt who slouched over a car magazine waiting for her to finish work. At least they had matching nails. With a final whiff of acetone she replaced the brush in the tiny bottle and stretched out her legs on the desk to let the polish dry. Was this really what she wanted to do for the rest of her life? What about the medical mercy missions she had dreamed about at med school? She'd completely forgotten about those until Steve mentioned it. Would she be any happier if she had done that? No car, no gym, no home … no James. Was it really James she was bored with? And what about Steve? What was he expecting tonight? For that matter, what was she expecting? Who was she kidding? Steve didn't do platonic. Can you scoop fire into your lap without your clothes getting burnt? Where had she heard that before? It sounded like something Mere would say.

It's just a harmless little drink. The thought soothed her. She slid into her shoes and adjusted her skirt. There was nothing wrong with having a couple of drinks. When was the last time she'd gone out for a drink after work? It sure beat going home to baked beans and television.

There was a knock at the door and Russell appeared filling the room with enthusiasm.

'Hey, Helene. Glad I caught you. I've a couple of things to discuss.' He motioned to the red couch. Was this good or bad? Had Lloyd told him that he'd seen her on the weekend with her 'husband'? She'd told Russell she was going alone.

'Nice stockings, by the way.' He grinned. 'I overheard a few comments in the waiting room this afternoon, all good, I can assure you!' He relaxed into the couch, stretched out his legs and clasped his hands behind his head. Helene sat opposite him, upright and uptight waiting for the worst.

'I heard you had a good weekend.'

This was it; he'd spoken to Lloyd. 'Very relaxing and the speakers were great. They organised it well.' How would she explain what she'd been doing?

'Yeah, he told me you were pretty wobbly on your feet.'

'Oh?' Her heart started to race. She couldn't think what to say. He knew and yet he looked so cool about it.

'I was pretty wobbly the first time too but it's a great sport.'

What was he talking about? Getting drunk and flirting was a great sport?

'I still do it – take the whole family with me when I can. I'm teaching my son to surf now.'

'Surfing. Of course.' It came out as almost a sigh of relief. He was talking about the conference's social program: food tour, golf or surfing. She had picked the surf lessons.

Russell gave her a puzzled look. 'Yeah, what did you think I meant?' His tone became serious. 'Helene you know you are one of my best doctors ...'

She crossed her legs and sat forward, instantly on edge again. Here it came – the telling off about how it didn't help the company image for a married doctor to be seen hanging off the arm of some random bloke. That it wasn't his business but could she please be more discreet.

'I had a chat to head office in Sydney today. They're reviewing their structure and a vacancy has come up. They want me to move to Sydney in the next few months to fill it.'

'Wow! Congratulations!' She almost jumped up and hugged him. This had nothing to do with her at all. 'Have you accepted?'

'Still discussing details with my wife but we've pretty much decided to go. So I need to replace myself. You know the company likes to recruit from within so I want to put your name forward. Do you reckon you're up for it?'

She could hardly believe what she was hearing. 'That's amazing! Thanks, Russell. I'm flattered.'

'I'm not flattering you. It makes good business sense. You're smart, young, attractive, and our corporate clients like you. That's the area we want to tap into, the corporate health market. That's where the money is. You'd be seeing our top execs a couple of days a week and the rest drumming up more business. And you'd need to do an MBA – part time of course.'

'I'm sure I could manage it. When do I need to let you know?'

'The sooner, the better. Head office wants it sorted by the end of the month. Talk it over with James. The job comes with plenty of corporate 'entertaining' so you'll be out quite a few nights each week. But I'm sure your thicker pay packet will compensate for not seeing each other so often.'

She still could not believe it as she dropped the nail varnish back on Mel's desk and took the lift to street level. She was bursting to call James and tell him but then she'd need to explain why she wasn't coming straight home. She joined the end of day bustle hurrying home past brightly lit shop windows and across impatient intersections. As she waited to cross a street clogged with cars she glimpsed a girl in a nearby shop. What a tart. The vermillion lips, the too short skirt, the towering heels, the black lace stockings… It was her – reflected in the shop's mirror! She stumbled sideways into a woman tapping out messages on her phone. It clattered to the ground.

'I'm so sorry.' She bent to pick it up, now acutely aware of her skirt scrunching even shorter. The lights changed, the traffic stopped and the pedestrians swarmed past her like water around a rock. What was she doing? She was no better than her father with his trashy tarts and pathetic promises. This was not the image she had slogged through medical school to create. This was not the behaviour of a trustworthy doctor about to become a senior manager. This was not the behaviour of a married woman. James might be boring but at least he was faithful. She turned around and headed home.

22

MERE
OKAHU BAY, AUCKLAND
1981

'I know.' How could those two tiny words have such power? Yet it wasn't the words themselves so much as the unspoken meaning that penetrated my defences and ricocheted my life in a new direction. It happened on a Sunday. I was thirty-five years old and in my third year at law school.

'Hurry up, you kids. Turn that TV off and put your shoes on. Dad's waiting.'

Good old Doug. What would I do without him? Every Sunday he took the kids out for the day so I could study. Usually it was church in the morning but not today; they were taking the ferry to Waiheke Island for a 'big adventure'. Even the older two, who usually preferred to hang out with their friends, were going. It would be good for them to spend some time with Doug and the younger kids. I cut the chunky corned beef sandwiches in half and squeezed them into a plastic container. The pack brimmed with food – sandwiches, a family pack of chocolate chip cookies, potato crisps and a two litre bottle of orange cordial. No doubt they would be quickly demolished by my five hungry teenagers who unfurled themselves from the saggy settee, rubbing their hands through thick waves of hair, scratching, stretching and yawning.

'Come here and give me a hug.'

They ambled into the kitchen, one after the other, wrapping their lithe arms around me.

'Bye, Mum.'

'Be good for your dad,' I told the younger ones. 'Keep an eye out for Derek and the twins,' I instructed the older ones.

'Yes, Mum.'

Their words were few but their lingering hugs spoke volumes. We were a happy family. Poor but happy. Doug was already revving up the engine of our rusty old Valiant. The kids piled in, making it slump even closer to the ground.

'See you tonight. Work hard.' He blew me a kiss.

The car stuttered down the hill. Like my joints, it took a while to warm up in the morning. I bent over to pull out a bunch of weeds that seemed to have sprung up overnight. They came out easily; shallow roots. If I left them alone long enough they would take over the whole garden, crowding out the original plants. A little regular weeding was all it took to allow the true plants to grow. Just one more year at law school and I would be that gardener, pulling out the weeds of our legal system and helping our people to flourish again.

Leaning on my ample thighs I levered myself upright. Hours of sitting and studying had done nothing to help my weight or the arthritis that thickened my knuckles like a seasoned boxer. I looked down the hill in time to see the Valiant disappear around the corner of Okahu Bay towards the city and the ferry terminal. Passing it in the opposite direction sped a motorbike. It turned right at the urupa and roared up the hill, only slowing at the last moment to turn onto the thin concrete strips of our driveway. Liz always rode her bike at top speed, the same way she lived life. She kicked the bike stand down and jumped off her bike with the agility of one of my kids, despite the heavy back pack she was wearing.

'Hi, Mere. Am I late? So sorry.' Her words tumbled out like her messy cascade of fair hair as she pulled off her helmet. She pulled an elastic band out of her jeans pocket and tied it up in a straight ponytail.

'You're not late at all. Doug and the kids have just left. Come on in.'

I led the way into the house with Liz jiggling out of her black leather jacket as we walked. Underneath she wore a bright orange tie dyed t-shirt with the words 'Ban the Boks' stamped across it. The South African rugby team had been and gone, leaving in its wake a nation, and even families, still divided, arguing over whether a country that practised apartheid should have been allowed to come. No one could agree, neither Maori nor Pakeha. Doug and I kept our views to ourselves. We could see both sides, but Liz proclaimed hers loud and clear.

'I'm dying for a coffee.' She dumped the pack on the worn floorboards and pulled out two thick tomes, a folder stuffed with pages and pages of scrawled notes and a packet of cameo cremes.

'Here you go,' she said, handing me the chocolate biscuits. 'Brain food.'

I tipped the biscuits on a chipped pink plate and made the coffee – black for Liz and white with five sugars for me.

'How can you drink it like that?' Liz smiled at me over her mug.

'How can you drink yours like that?' We had only got to know each other this year but since working together on this moot we were rapidly becoming good friends.

Liz opened her note folder and pulled out a wad of pages. 'I've been researching Judge Acheson. Have you heard of him? He was a judge of the native land court in the twenties and thirties. Very pro Maori.'

'A Pakeha judge defending Maori land rights? There can't have been too many of them around back then.'

'There weren't.'

'That would be right.' I couldn't help the bitterness that regurgitated every so often in my thoughts and speech. It would take me by surprise, like a lurking stomach bug, rising up and spewing out with little warning.

Liz sifted through her notes. 'Yeah. He was way ahead of his time. From what I've read he was a real spoke in the established wheels of justice. My kind of bloke. Look at this.'

She stabbed enthusiastically at a scrawled paragraph highlighted with yellow. 'In these claims over Maori rights to these lakes up north he insisted on taking 'judicial notice' of the Treaty of Waitangi, which was totally radical at the time. It sets a precedent we can use for our case.'

We worked all morning, poring over our books and notes, checking and rechecking references and arguing until we agreed. Land law was our passion, unlike the younger students whose passions lay more with each other than the subject.

'That's it, we're finished.' Liz leaned back and stretched her freckled arms behind her. 'I think we deserve a break. Do you feel like a walk?'

The sky was clear. It was a beautiful afternoon. A walk was just what we needed to refresh ourselves before practising our speeches. We finished off yet another cup of coffee and the final few cameo cremes, then set off down the hill towards the bay. Liz wrinkled up her thin nose, inhaling the fresh air and tilting her head back with child-like delight.

'Where are Doug and the kids? I hope they're enjoying this sunshine while it lasts.'

'They've gone to Waiheke for the day, lucky things. I'd love to see what it's like.'

'That's where I grew up,' Liz replied. 'It has bittersweet memories for me.'

We walked through the playground past a mum and dad pushing their two daughters on the swings. Liz glanced at them and continued.

'We were just like that: Mum, Dad and us two girls. We had such fun together playing at the beach, the playground, in the bush, but mostly out on the boat. I remember the time we went out to greet the Queen as she sailed up the harbour on her visit. Mum had decorated the boat with red, white and blue paper streamers and Dad rigged up the Union Jack. There were hundreds of boats. I remember Mum and Dad laughing and hugging and yelling out "God save the Queen" at the top of their voices. We were all so happy, until Mum died.'

'I'm so sorry. How old were you?'

'Twelve, and Maggie, my sister, was ten. Everything changed. Dad cried for weeks and then he started drinking.'

'I know what that's like. My dad was just the same when my brother died.'

Liz nodded in empathy. 'I don't think you ever really get over it.' Her tears magnified the blueness of her eyes. She continued. 'It wasn't too bad during the week because he knew he had to stay sober in the boat – he was a fisherman. But every Saturday night he would leave us with the neighbour and come into town. He brought us with him once. We all slept on the boat, right out there.' She pointed at the small bay dotted with anchored boats. 'He really loved us. He called us his little princesses.'

She smiled at me and I felt an uneasy stirring in my stomach. By now we had reached Tamaki Drive. We waited for a line of traffic to pass, then crossed the road to the beach. We took off our shoes and walked along the warm sand.

'So where is your dad now?' I asked.

'He died a few years ago. I hadn't seen him for years. When he lost his boat he lost his livelihood. He eventually found a good job in the South Island and after that we hardly ever saw him.'

'Why didn't you go with him? Why did he leave you here?'

'He thought it was for the best. A fishing trawler is no place for two girls.'

'So where did you live?'

'The neighbour offered to look after us. Dad sent her money every month to feed and care for us but she kept most of it. She made me and my sister sleep in a shed at the far end of the garden.'

'A shed, do you mean like a garden shed?' I was horrified.

'Yes. We had a threadbare rug on the concrete floor, a single bed each and a chest of drawers sandwiched between the lawnmower and a pile of paint tins. It was freezing in winter and leaked when it rained.'

'You'd lost your mum and your dad, and she stuck you out there? How could anyone be that cruel? Didn't you get sick?'

'Constantly. Then she would tell us off and complain that Dad didn't send her enough money for stuff like doctor's bills. But I knew Dad sent her plenty.'

'Why didn't he take you out of there?'

'We always told him that everything was fine so he wouldn't worry. We were scared he might start drinking even more. We were scared we would lose him.' She picked up a shell and tossed it in the water

I couldn't believe what I was hearing. More than that, I didn't want to believe it. The uneasy stirring in my stomach had escalated to the violent flip-flopping of a snared fish. Her dad had 'lost' his boat. Surely it couldn't have been here, in this bay? Surely it hadn't been her dad's boat that I had burned? I had to know, I dreaded to know. My legs felt like lead weights. We had reached the end of the small bay, where the beach tapered off into a bank of large rocks. We sat down and looked out past the anchored boats and bobbing kayaks to the harbour, its water ruffled by the many Sunday sailors. A cold gust of wind rushed across the bay and hit us straight in the face. My lungs felt tight as though gripped in a vice. I could hardly breathe. I had to know. I forced the words out. 'How did your Dad lose his boat?' I couldn't look at her.

Liz's voice was still and quiet behind me. 'It was burned.'

Her words hung in the air, suspended between us like an enormous, black bomb. I couldn't move. I couldn't breathe. I wanted to shrink into the sand, disappear, escape. Then I felt her hand on my shoulder, gentle and strangely calming, and then the words I will never forget: 'I know.'

If she had shown even a trace of anger I could have fought back, justified my actions, defended myself. But her voice held no condemnation, only sadness and love. Like a sudden landslide those two words ripped away my righteous anger exposing the guilt that it had masked for so many years. The full weight of it blanketed my body. My hand clutched at my greenstone pendent and Rewiti's fishing sinker. I couldn't see for the tears that filled my eyes. I choked out a word: 'How?'

'Dad saw you. He was walking back from the city and saw the flames. By the time he arrived here it was too late. He saw you sitting up there.' She pointed to where the flax bushes had once lined the beach.

'Why didn't he tell the police? Wasn't he furious?'

'Of course he was furious. He told us his first instinct was to race over and give you a good belting. But he was sober enough to know that would do more harm than good. He'd already had a few run-ins with the cops. He got close enough to hear you crying, and he understood. Some of his drinking buddies were from around here. Despite his short temper and weakness for the bottle, Dad was one of the most compassionate men I have ever met. The police said it was an accident anyway. He kept quiet and claimed the paltry insurance.'

'But it ruined your lives. I never thought ...' My voice caught in my throat.

'That's the way I looked at it for many years. If only Dad hadn't lost his boat, if only we were all still together. I wanted to hate you. But I eventually realised that Dad's way was right. If I held onto my anger it would paralyse my life. He always said that we can't control what happens but we can control how we react to it. I would never have had the drive to become a lawyer, to defend the rights of those who cannot defend themselves, without going through those tough times.'

'But how did you know it was me?'

Liz laughed. 'I sure knew your name because Dad made us say it every day.'

'How would he have known that?' I was dumbfounded.

'After you left the beach he decided to sleep there until morning. There was nothing else he could do. When he woke up you were all having church on the beach. He recognised you and heard someone call your name. He wasn't a religious man – never set foot in a church that I know of – but he had this thing about praying for his enemies. He would often do it just before he hit them. Well you were our enemy so we had to pray for you. I can tell you, those prayers weren't too nice to start with but they mellowed over the years. It was still a shock to find you in my law class. I expected to feel that old anger but it had disappeared.'

She took my hand. 'Mere, you are a good person. I wanted to tell you this so we can be friends, with no secrets between us.'

I looked at her thin freckled hand clasping my plump, brown one. 'How can you hold no grudge? Why would you want to be my friend? I burnt your Dad's boat.' After all these years of keeping silent, it was a relief, in a strange way, to admit it out loud. But it didn't alleviate the shame.

'Silly! Who else am I going to do my assignments with? Us two old bags have to stick together.' She shook my hand playfully.

'Mature is the word.' We were back to our usual repartee.

'Speak for yourself. Mature sounds boring; I'd rather be a crazy old bag.' She jumped up and whirled around, arms outspread and hair flying. 'Come on, you old bag, get off that rock and let's go finish that speech.'

***

The guilt weighed heavy on me. Liz seemed oblivious to it. That made it almost worse. As soon as she had sped off on her bike, I sank down at the kitchen table, dropping my head into my hands. My joints ached. I felt sapped of energy. All these years I had been almost proud of what I had got away with, any sense of shame or guilt obliterated by my righteous anger. It had been an act of utu (at least my limited understanding of it), payback for ruining my life, but all I had done was ruin someone else's. I stretched my hands out in despair. They touched something – a book. I looked up. It was Doug's bible. He often left it lying around. I pulled it towards me and opened it at random. Perhaps God would speak to me? It was a vain hope – why would He? I had never spoken to Him. I started reading the words on the page out loud: *When I kept silent my bones wasted away through my groaning all day long. For day and night your hand was heavy upon me; my strength was sapped as in the heat of summer. Then I acknowledged my sin to you … and you forgave the guilt of my sin.*

My heart beat faster. That was exactly how I felt: my bones wracked with arthritis, my strength sapped. Could it be that easy? Could I get rid of this weight of guilt simply by acknowledging it to God? What did I have to lose by trying? I put my hands together in some attempt at reverence as I fumbled for the right words to say. Dad and Doug were so much better at this sort of thing than me.

'Dear Lord.' It sounded so awkward. 'I'm really sorry.'

I waited. Would He forgive me? How would I know? Silence. I rubbed my lips. They felt sort of hot. Not as hot as the time I mistook chilli for capsicum but definitely hot. Then a gust of wind blew through the open window flicking over the pages of the bible to Isaiah. Dad had often referred to Isaiah in his talks to the people on Bastion Point. The words on the page seemed to jump out at me.

Then one of the seraphs flew to me with a live coal in his hand, which he had taken with tongs from the altar. With it he touched my mouth and said, 'See, this has touched your lips; your guilt is taken away and your sin atoned for.'

The minutes ticked away in silence until gradually the heat on my lips disappeared. I sat up straight. It might have been my imagination but I felt a lot better, somehow lighter. I looked up at the clock. It wasn't yet five. Doug and the kids wouldn't be home for another hour. I turned over the pages of the bible, towards the back. If God was really speaking to me, would He have anything else to say? The words before me were familiar, a reminder of Sunday School all those years ago. As though highlighted with Liz's yellow marker one line stood out: … *as we forgive those who sin against us*. Now that was a problem. I looked over at the bunch of positive thinking books lined up on the bookshelf. I had tried to take their advice about forgiving but it wasn't as easy as they made out. That bitter anger had roots as tangled and stubborn as the pohutukawa trees that clung to the steep cliffs around the headland. I raised my eyes heavenwards.

'I can't do it. I've tried. Please could you help me?'

I learned that day that the power of words is not in their number or even their literal meaning. The power comes from the heart that forms them.

∽

23

JAMES

James dumped his keys and mobile on the hall table and headed for the bedroom. He stripped off his clothes and pulled on his running gear. It was good to get home while there was still a hint of daylight. He'd sent off the Silver Service project and received the thumbs up by return e-mail. These one-off projects were good but it was the promise of ongoing work that would set his business on a more solid footing. The contract with Bob was just getting the legal check-up before the final signing. Between that and this work with Nicolette's public relations company he'd be sitting pretty. Her boss had liked what he'd sent through yesterday and wanted to meet tonight. It seemed a bit rushed but she was off to Indonesia tomorrow for a couple of weeks and wanted it sorted before she went. Fair enough. The sooner the better as far as he was concerned. Nicolette's phone call had been brisk and to the point without a hint of anything else. They would make a good team if she would stick to business only. The meeting was at seven but she couldn't give him a place until she had confirmed with her boss. He was still waiting for the text. Meanwhile, he figured he could fit in a quick ten kilometre run. He pulled on his running shoes and headed out the front door. Mere was walking up the driveway.

'Hi, Mere. You're all dressed up. Have you been out?'

'Yes! An old friend of mine from university days took me to lunch. We caught the City Cat to New Farm, to a lovely Italian delicatessen, and looked around the museum there by the river. You know, the one that used to be an old powerhouse. Fascinating. Then we went to Southbank to the art gallery. I love the Aboriginal designs; quite different from Maori art.' She coughed.

'It sounds as though you've had a busy day. Mum didn't tell me you'd been to university. What did you study?'

'Law.'

'So that explains all those thick books in your room. Are you still practising?'

'I help out now and then, when I'm needed. That's another reason I came here. At home, I just can't say no when they ask me to help.'

'Well you are sure helping us. The garden has never looked so good.'

'Your garden is easy – just a few weeds to pull out and some pruning. I enjoy it.' She coughed again, hunching over with the spasm.

'Are you okay?' James asked.

'She straightened up and cleared her throat. 'I'm fine, dear. Just a little tired, that's all.'

'Well, take care of yourself. Maybe you'd like to have lunch with us this weekend. I'm sure Helene isn't busy.'

'That would be lovely but I'm going up to see your parents this weekend. Shirley and I arranged it this morning. It's a bit last minute but it's less than two weeks until I go back to New Zealand.'

'That's gone quickly. I'm sure you will have a great time with Mum. She's probably spent all day cooking.'

'I'm not surprised. We both grew up learning that you can never have too much food for your guests.' Mere patted her stomach and they shared a laugh. He headed up the road, his long legs striding out in a loping gait.

Forty-five minutes later he raced through the front door, grabbed his phone on the way to the shower and checked his messages. Yes – one from Nicolette. It read: West End Wine Bar 7pm. He dropped the phone on the bed, stripped off his sweaty clothes and jumped into the shower. He didn't want to be late to meet a new potential client. With his still damp hair dripping on his t-shirt he jumped in the car and sped off. He was stopped at a red light when he remembered that he hadn't told Helene he would be late. He slid his hand into his jeans pocket but his phone wasn't there. Damn. He must have left it at home. Too bad; she wouldn't expect him home before eight anyway. The meeting wouldn't take that long. He parked the car in a side street and cut across the tiny park to the main street. It was busy for a Thursday night with people queuing up for take-out dinners while others staggered home with grocery bags banging against their legs. The wine bar was packed with people starting their weekend early. He sidestepped a waiter balancing a tray of generously filled wine glasses and scanned the buzzing tables for Nicolette. In the far corner he saw her in earnest discussion with another woman. Both were dressed in suits and high heels. He squeezed through the crowd.

'James!' Nicolette twirled her glass of wine. 'So glad you could make it at such short notice. Let me introduce my boss, Barb.'

Barb stood up and leaned over the table to shake his hand. Her suit was fitting and her perfume hit him like a head-high tackle.

'So finally I get to meet the man behind the designs.'

Her mascara-laden eyes performed a practiced sweep of his clothes while her smile crinkled her tanned face like thick brown paper. Her eyes and forehead remained eerily smooth.

'We were just discussing your work. We're very impressed. Please,' she beckoned to the spare chair, 'sit down and relax. Wine?'

'Beer, thanks.'

She clicked her fingers in the air at a passing waiter. 'Waiter!' Her voice was imperious and he responded accordingly, taking the drinks order and scurrying away. It was embarrassing.

She pulled out a file of papers and clicked her pen.

'Right, let's get down to business. Nicolette's told you I'm off to Indonesia next week and we have some urgent work that needs doing while I'm away.'

'I thought you were off tomorrow. Wasn't that why we had to meet –'

Nicolette interrupted with a laugh. 'No, no, it's next week. You must have misheard. Anyway, the sooner we sign you up the better.'

'Absolutely,' gushed Barb. 'We're keen to get our hands on you. You have no idea how difficult it is to find good graphic designers.'

He should have felt flattered but instead he felt as though he'd walked into a spider's web. The beer arrived. It tasted terrible in his freshly tooth-brushed mouth.

'What exactly do you need?' He wanted to keep this meeting strictly professional.

Barb riffled through the pile of papers and pulled out a couple.

'We have two urgent jobs that the ad agency didn't finish. They need to be done by the end of next week.'

She pushed the papers towards him. He picked them up and scanned the two job briefs. One was a program layout for a film festival and the other was a series of designs to promote an upcoming fashion show.

Barb smoothed a sun-spotted hand over her spiky peroxide highlights. 'The film festival should be simple but for the fashion show we want something special – something that encapsulates the essence of Queensland. You know: sun, sea, rainforest without the clichés.' She waved her hand poetically around as she spoke.

'We could go with dirt, mining and heavy machinery. It's one of Queensland's major income producers.'

Nicolette spluttered on her wine. Barb's hand stopped in mid-air. They looked like two stunned mullets, although mullets probably didn't have such bright red lips.

'I don't think that's quite what we had in mind.' Nicolette was the first to regain speech but Barb interrupted her.

'Actually …' She stared, unfocussed, at the bar, her mind obviously churning through imaginative possibilities. Then her hand started up again.

'Heavy machinery, drills, hard hats, work boots, the hard grit of the real Queensland … I love it!' She looked at her watch. 'I must run, darlings. I've got dinner at eight with the Minister of Sports.' She stood up and shook his hand.

'James, it's great to have you on board. I'll leave you in Nicolette's capable hands. She'll sort out the tedious admin details, won't you darling? I'll see you in the morning. About ten.'

They air kissed each other on both cheeks and Barb swirled off through the crowd.

Nicolette grinned at James.

'I knew she would like you. And this idea for the fashion show, it's so original.'

She placed her hand on his as it lay on the table, one finger stroking the side of his hand. 'You're so talented. Has anyone told you that?'

Her words were like honey. No one that mattered had told him that; neither his parents nor Helene. It felt good.

She continued in a low voice. He leaned a little closer to hear her above the surrounding music and chatter. 'I don't think you realise just how much you have going for you. I bet you haven't even noticed that half the women in this bar keep looking at you.'

'I'm just here for the work. If I need a woman to look at me I've got Helene.' He moved to pull his hand away but she held on.

'Really? And when was the last time she looked at you? I mean, really looked at you. Like this.' She leaned towards him, holding his gaze and his hand, until their lips met. She darted her tongue between his teeth. He knew he should pull away but he couldn't. He felt mesmerised and yet irked at the same time. Did she really think he was that weak? That he would so easily fall into bed with her? It wasn't as if he hadn't imagined it. It had taken him ages to focus on his work after she had left yesterday. And that was the trouble. He didn't need that sort of drama distracting him from his work. The next few months were critical for the business. He needed to put a dampener on it, and fast.

'Nic, you know you're incredibly attractive. Any man would want you. But I'm here for work, not play.'

'Oh.' Her voice dripped with mock disappointment.

'I was thinking more of a package deal. Barb provides the work and I provide the play. Haven't you heard the saying: All work and no play makes James a dull boy?' She laughed lightly as though they were discussing the weather. He tried to keep his reply light also.

'Thanks for the offer but I'll have to pass. Did Barb mention some paperwork?' he asked, trying to pull the conversation back to safer ground.

'Just our standard contract for the two jobs.' She handed them to him.

'I'll take a look tonight and get them back to you tomorrow.'

'Fine. Now I do have a little favour to ask.' She finished off her wine. 'Could you drop me home? I walked to work this morning and caught a lift over here with Barb.'

He was just congratulating himself on handling a potentially sticky situation and now she needed a ride home. He couldn't say no. Oh well, a ride was no big deal and he needed to keep his newest client at least partly happy.

'Sure. My car's on the other side of the park over there.'

They walked down the street. Nicolette tucked her arm in his and leant on him.

'I think the wine has made me a little light-headed. I should have had some lunch. How about we pick up a pizza?'

He steadied her as they crossed the road.

'I need to get home. Helene will probably be wondering where I am.'

'I doubt it.'

Their footsteps crunched on the gravel path that led through the unlit park. What did she mean by that?

Nicolette gripped tighter onto his arm. 'It's dark in here.'

He looked up at the solitary park light positioned near a park bench. 'Looks as though it's been smashed. Steady there.'

Nicolette stumbled on the loose gravel. He caught her. The movement spun her round to face him, their faces inches apart. She snaked her arms around his neck and tried to kiss him.

'No, Nicolette. I didn't mean it like that.' He stepped backwards and stumbled over the raised edge of the path. Nicolette clung on as they tumbled to the ground. She landed on top and started kissing his chest, his throat, his neck. She slid her hand down over his jeans. Her breath was hot against his ear. 'I knew there was a real man hiding in there. Come on, loosen up and have some fun. Helene will never know.'

'Won't I?' If someone had doused him with icy water it wouldn't have been more of a shock. The voice was like frozen steel. She stood above them like that Amazon goddess he had first encountered in Southbank, only this time she wasn't smiling.

24

The first thing Helene noticed when she walked into the bedroom was the mess. Sweaty running gear trailed from the bed to the bathroom. She scooped up the clothes and dumped them in the white cane laundry basket, empty thanks to Mere. It was only as she walked back through the bedroom on the way to the kitchen that she noticed James' mobile abandoned on the bed. He must have forgotten it in his obvious hurry to get somewhere, but where? It was unusual enough for him to have come home early and even more unusual for him to go out again without letting her know. Perhaps he'd just popped out to pick up some dinner. But weren't the leftovers of all that Thai food he had brought home last night still in the fridge? She picked up his phone and searched messages. The most recent was only a few hours ago. She opened it and felt her legs go weak beneath her. Her heart thumped as she read it again: 'West End Wine Bar 7pm'. The message itself was innocent enough; he often met clients at cafes or pubs. But what was the meaning of that single red rose at the end of the message and no name or number? Surely he wouldn't be meeting someone romantically, would he? Who was this red rose woman? That could explain the late nights at work. He wasn't like that though - or was he? Had she been so busy 'taking control', as Nicolette had put it, that she'd missed the signs? And all that 'putting it out to the universe' rubbish. All it had got her was an embarrassing mess. She didn't want Steve, or anyone else for that matter. She wanted James. She wanted to kill him. What was he doing over at that wine bar?

Face flushed, mind whirling, she marched to the car, started it up and slammed it into reverse. The car charged out of the driveway. If there were any cars coming they would just have to give way, she was in no mood for niceties. That red rose. Who could it be? She should have checked for other messages. What were they doing at the wine bar? Would they still be there? She shoved her foot on the accelerator, speeding through the amber traffic lights. If a cop dared to try and pull her over, look out, she would snap his head off, just like she would snap off that red rose. In a frenzied haze, she somehow ended up at West End and parked on the street a few hundred metres from the wine bar. An icy calm settled over her. She smacked on some lip gloss and smoothed her stockings. She was an 'in control' career woman, not some mousy, jilted wife. She stalked into the wine bar and perched on a stool in a dark corner of the bar, crossing her lacy stockinged legs.

'What can I get ya, babe?' The bartender grinned at her. She tried not to cringe.

'Champagne, thanks, and do you have any cigarettes?'

'No smoking in here and sorry we don't sell them. But ...' he stared at her lacy stockings 'you can have one of mine if you sit outside. I'll find you a table.'

She glanced around. Were they still here?

'Never mind, I don't really need it. Just the champagne will be fine.'

She hadn't felt like smoking since the stress of med school, or to be more exact, the stress of Steve. At least that was out of her system. But now this. She peered through the crowds, searching each table. It was difficult to see but wasn't that Nicolette in the far corner smiling and holding hands across the table with ... with James. It couldn't be. She stared at the two of them chatting so intimately. Then Nicolette leaned forward and they kissed. It felt like a jab of anaesthetic; a sharp sting, then numbness. This couldn't be happening. Nicolette and James? Nic was meant to be her friend and James – wasn't he the loyal, trustworthy, boring one? From what she could see he didn't look either boring or bored. The bartender handed her a glass of champagne. She skulled it.

'I thought you were meant to savour the expensive stuff,' he joked.

'I'm thirsty.' She tried to be civil.

'Can I get you another?' he asked.

She looked across the room. They were leaving.

'No thanks. I have to go.' She pulled a twenty dollar note from her wallet and left it on the bar.

'Hey, don't you want your change?' the bartender called after her.

'You keep it.' Trying to look casual, she hurried after them. They were walking down the street, arm in arm. She felt sick and it wasn't just the champagne on an empty stomach. They crossed the road and headed towards the park. She stepped out between two parked cars. A car swerved to avoid her. 'Hey, watch where you're going!' an angry voice shouted out the window. If he'd stopped she would have punched a dent in his precious Porsche. They had disappeared. She crossed the road and hurried along the dim path to catch them up. She didn't want to lose them in the dark. No chance of that. There they were writhing on the grass, in full view of anyone who walked past. How pathetic. She tip-toed closer. Nicolette was whispering something in James' ear.

'Come on, loosen up and have some fun. Helene will never know.'

The bloody tart. She could snap off her silly stilettos right now and shove them … No, she wouldn't lower herself to their level. She stood over them as though they were a couple of tiny squirming insects and steeled her voice.

'Won't I?'

The effect was instant. It might even have been funny if it hadn't been so horrible. James pushed Nicolette away and jumped to his feet. 'Helene! We were. I was –'

'I can see very well what you were doing.'

Nicolette still lay on the grass, propped up on her elbows, her legs crossed casually in front as though she was at a picnic. She didn't even look embarrassed.

'Helene, what a surprise. I thought you would still be with … what's his name?'

Her words felt like poison darts.

'Well I'm not,' she snapped.

'With who?' James asked.

She glared at him. 'This is about you two, not me.'

Nicolette wiped her mouth. 'We've done nothing wrong.'

'Nothing wrong! What would you call it? An accident?

James grabbed her hand. 'Helene, it's not what it seems. I can explain.'

She pushed him away, the icy veneer starting to crack. 'Don't even try to explain. I never want to see you, or her, again.' She went to pull off her wedding ring to fling on the ground but her finger was barren. That would be right. This marriage had been on the rocks for ages. She spun on her heel and walked away, tears scalding her eyes.

James ran up beside her. 'Let me drive you home. You're in no state to drive.'

'And you're in no state to speak to me. Go back to that tart. You're obviously busy.'

'We're not busy. It's nothing. She's nothing.'

'It didn't look like nothing to me.'

'Helene, stop!' He grabbed her arm. She wrenched it away.

'How could you?' She smeared the tears off her face.

'Are ya okay, luv?' A thick-set bloke in a muscle shirt came up to them on the footpath. 'Do ya need me to sort 'im out?' He nodded his dreadlocked head at James.

'I'm her husband.' She had never heard James sound so violent.

'Righto. Take good care of her mate.' She half expected him to add, 'or I'll …' who knows what a bloke that size could do?

Some busybodies had gathered over the road to watch the drama. Didn't they have anything better to do? She didn't need to air her dirty washing in public. James must have been thinking the same.

'Let's talk about this in private. If you're sure you're okay to drive, I'll meet you at home.'

'Okay.' It was like the final puff from a deflated balloon. She turned away and trudged to the car. As she opened the door she saw James jog straight past Nicolette who was standing at the edge of the park, throwing a few words at her as he passed. She stood there, hands on hips, calling after him, 'What about me?'

At least he hadn't stopped. Perhaps it was true what he'd said. But she couldn't shake that awful image of them rolling around in the grass together. And then there was what Nicolette had said. She would have to explain that to James. Would he be any less hurt than she was about him? She thought about Noosa. Had he done anything worse than she?

Tears spilled down her cheeks. She smeared them away. She could hardly see to drive. It was such a mess.

***

It all happened so fast. One minute she was rounding the corner at the bottom of the hill, the next she had hit the kerb. The car flipped upside down and skidded on its roof straight into a tree. The impact righted the car with a shuddering jolt. Her whole body jarred with the impact. She felt like the front windscreen – completely shattered. Her foot hurt and something warm trickled down the side of her face. Her breathing was shallow and rapid. Bile rose in her throat. She was going into shock. She had to get out.

Helene unlatched the seat belt and tried to move. A spear of pain shot through her foot. It was jammed under the crumpled steering column. She touched her hand to her forehead. It came away covered with blood. The crushed roof pressed on her head adding to the throbbing pain. It felt as though it would burst. She was trapped.

'Helene!' Through the shattered glass she saw James running towards the car. She saw the horror on his face and heard the panic in his voice. 'Helene, thank God you're alive. Are you alright?' He tried to prise open the car door but it would not budge.

'I can't move my legs; they're stuck.' Her tongue felt like a slab of steak in her mouth, mangling the words as she tried to talk.

He pulled off his t-shirt and squeezed it through the partially open driver's window. 'Here, press this to your head.'

She manoeuvred her arm in the cramped space and took the shirt blotting the blood that was still flowing freely down her face. Head wounds always bled a lot. The knowledge didn't reassure her. She pressed the blood soaked shirt harder against her head and winced. James fumbled for his phone.

'Damn, I left it at home!' He ran his hands through his hair, pacing the pavement in the darkness. 'Just stay there. I'll run for help.'

Helene lay still, explosions of pain ricocheting from her head to her foot. She was helplessly sandwiched. Oh, to go to sleep. She closed her eyes. Is this how Granddad had felt as he lay trapped? Had he shut his eyes and drifted into death? She could see his stoved in chest, the internal organs punctured, his life draining away. She could see the newspaper clippings spread across her grandmother's kitchen table; a morbid memorial to how her beloved husband had died.

Flying doctor dies after plane hits kangaroo.

The locals had clustered around the smashed plane, helpless to do anything except wait for another plane to make the two hour trip to the remote landing strip. It was too late. She squeezed her eyes in pain, overwhelmed by the grief she thought had long since abated. Granddad had lived and died helping others. What if she died tonight? What would her life have counted for? Had she made a difference? What would the papers say: Doctor dies in car crash after arguing with husband? Was that the sum of her life?

She heard the distant sound of sirens. Help was on its way, help that her granddad had deserved so much more than her.

A flashlight shone in her face, glowing through her still closed eyes.

'Are you all right, miss?' She forced her heavy lids to open. A policeman peered through the window.

'I'm okay, I think, but I'm stuck.'

' Hold tight. We'll get you out.'

She closed her eyes again. She was so tired. Too tired to care about the deafening crunching and cracking of metal as they extricated her from the car. Finally, the noise stopped. She heard voices commanding, chatting, coming closer.

'Hi, Helene. I'm one of the ambulance officers. I'm just going to check you out before we move you.' He gently lifted the blood soaked shirt from her head then pressed her hand back onto it.

'You've done a good job there. The bleeding's almost stopped. Can you keep your hand there for me?'

His voice was calm, soothing, in control. She opened her eyes and looked at his broad friendly face. He was an older man. His face, his voice, reminded her of her granddad. She felt safe. He scooped his arms under her legs and lifted her carefully away from the car, laying her on a waiting stretcher. James crouched beside her, his broad bare chest just inches from her face. The kindly ambulance officer replaced the sodden shirt with fresh packing gauze and directed James to hold it in place. Then he returned his attention to Helene.

'Have you had anything to drink this evening?'

'Just a glass of champagne.' The words wavered out.

'When did you last eat?'

'I had a banana and a coffee for lunch. Nothing since then.' The thought of food made her nauseous. She desperately wanted water. Her foot and head throbbed and her vision started to go black.

'I think I'm going to faint.'

James grasped her hand. 'It's all right. Everything will be all right.'

His voice sounded so distant, like a dream …

The slam of the ambulance door brought her round. Her eyes fluttered open to see her granddad perched over her. Her vision cleared. No it wasn't him; it was the ambulance officer.

'Where's James? Didn't he come with us?' She felt strangely fragile. The tears so violently interrupted by the accident threatened to overwhelm her again. She wanted James near her.

'He's following in his car.'

She lay back exhausted and let the tears flow.

25

The morning after the accident Helene woke late. She'd had little sleep the night before; a few short hours interrupted every thirty minutes by the medical staff monitoring the severity of concussion. They had finally discharged her early this morning. Her own bed had never felt so good. Her eyes squinted at the sun streaming through the bedroom window. The movement pulled at the stitches in her forehead. She sat up and looked at her foot bound firmly in a crepe bandage. Her toes looked like puffy little red sausages. The x-ray had shown no fractures but that didn't mean that one of the tiny bones in the foot wasn't broken. If it didn't settle she would need weight bearing x-rays and perhaps an MRI to confirm whether it was just a sprain. Just a sprain! They were often worse than fractures and this one would have her stuck on her bed for a week and hobbling in a cumbersome boot for the next two at least. When was the last time she had been a patient? Now the boot was on the other foot, so to speak, she wasn't sure she liked it. But her physical state was nothing compared with the turmoil in her mind. James' concerned looks and the protective arm he laid over her as they fell asleep last night told her he still cared but it didn't gel with what she had seen.

James had some explaining to do but she did too. What should she tell him about Steve? He was bound to ask after what Nicolette had said. So much for friendship. Her head throbbed. She pushed the sheets aside and hobbled to the bathroom. She would feel much better once she was up and dressed. She turned the shower to hot and let it soothe her aching body. She couldn't really expect to smash into a tree without suffering at least a few aches and pains.

'You're lucky to be alive.' Both the police officer and the ambulance guys had said it. And the accident and emergency registrar, as he stitched her head, had repeated the saying she often thought herself: 'Someone must be looking after you.'

Freshly dressed, bed made and her foot re-bandaged, she lay back on her bed with her foot elevated on a pile of pillows and her iPad in hand. She had nothing to do all day except check her e-mails and the latest medical journals. Or perhaps just worry and sleep.

There was a tap at the door and Mere appeared.

'Hello, dearie. James popped in on his way to work and told me all about the accident. How are you feeling?'

'A bit battered but I guess that's to be expected.'

'Of course it is. James said you were very lucky, although I am sure you don't feel like that at the moment. Have you had anything to eat this morning?'

'I'm not really hungry.'

'Nonsense. You need a bit of food in your belly to help you mend. How about I make you a nice cup of tea and some toast and marmalade?'

'I don't think we have marmalade but there is jam.' The talk of food started her stomach grumbling. 'Thank you, Mere. That would be lovely.'

She heard Mere singing as she bustled around the kitchen. The smell of cooked toast wafted into the bedroom, followed not long afterwards by Mere carrying a teapot, her favourite fine china cup and a plate of toast smothered in apricot jam.

'There you go. You get that down you and you'll feel a lot better. I'm going to hang out the washing and tidy up. Then I'll be back to check on you.'

'Thanks so much, Mere, but what about your book? I don't want to distract you from your writing.'

'My book can wait. When there's a choice between work and people, the work can always wait.'

Her grin was infectious. Helene felt brighter. It was nice to have someone around. She took a bite of her toast and opened up her e-mails. There was one from James sent at seven this morning.

'Hope you are feeling okay. I didn't want to wake you this morning. I have some stuff to sort out at work but should be back later this afternoon. I love you but we need to talk …'

He loved her but …? It sounded ominous. She hit 'reply'.

'Just woke up. Feel okay. Mere brought me breakfast.'

How should she sign it? She didn't want him to think she would just forgive and forget last night; that a simple 'I love you' would sort it all out. Did he really mean it or was it just another trite marital cliché? When she thought about him with Nicolette she hated him. Yet the thought of losing him pulled at her heart far worse than the stitches in her head. She typed 'Love, Helene' and hit 'send'.

It was early afternoon when Mere appeared lugging a brimming laundry basket.

'Would you like some company? I thought I might do the ironing in here.'

'I can't let you do all our housework, Mere.'

'It's the least I can do to repay your hospitality. And it gives me space to think about my family.'

Helene switched off her iPad. She had read enough medical journals for one day.

'Tell me about your family. How many children do you have? Was it five?'

'Five children, nineteen grandchildren and two great grandchildren. I'm missing those young ones, being over here. They are good at coming to see their old nanny.'

'So they all live near you?'

'Most of them. My daughter and her family live in London at the moment, and my eldest, Paul, lives in Wellington. I see him every few months when I'm down there.'

'What takes you to Wellington so often?'

'I help out on a few committees down there.'

'What type of committees?' The local bowls or church committee wouldn't take her all the way down to New Zealand's capital city.

'The main one is the Waitangi Tribunal. It looks at Maori issues of justice and upholding the Treaty of Waitangi.'

'That sounds important. I thought you were just a …' She stopped, embarrassed at her words.

'Just a housewife?' Mere finished off. She smiled. 'That was my first and most important job. It wasn't until the kids were at school that I decided to study law. It was hard for them, and for me. I missed out on a lot of their growing up, but my husband, Doug, and my sister and parents were always there for them.'

'What made you do law?' She was fascinated to find out more and mortified that she had judged her so blithely. Mere's life was far from what she had assumed.

'The history of my people is one of battling the law. During the five hundred and six days on Bastion Point I realised that if we didn't understand the laws of the country we had no way of changing them. I wanted to be able to help my people fight for justice, without violence.'

'Bastion Point? What is that? I've never heard of it.'

The front door opened. James was home.

Mere turned off the iron and hung the last few shirts in the wardrobe.

'I'll tell you all about it next week. Now here's your lovely husband and that's the cue for me to go and pack my bags. I have to be at the train station at five.'

'Where are you going?' Helene asked.

'Shirley invited me up for the weekend. They're meeting me off the train tonight. I'll be back Monday afternoon. You look after yourself and make sure you get some rest.'

She picked up the empty laundry basket and hurried out. Helene called after her.

'Have a good weekend.'

She was already looking forward to hearing more of Mere's story. She heard James and Mere chatting in the hallway. After a few moments James wandered in and perched awkwardly on the edge of the bed. She braced herself as he started to speak.

'I'm really sorry about what's happened with Nicolette but you have to believe me, there is nothing in it.'

'So how do you explain last night?'

'She offered me work. They've lost their ad agency and asked me to take over for them. It would have been a good deal with steady work. Nicolette arranged for me to meet her boss last night. That's what I was doing at the wine bar. Her boss left and Nicolette asked me to drive her home.'

'Didn't look like driving her home to me. I saw you kiss her in the bar, not to mention that pathetic display in the park.'

'She kissed me. I didn't kiss her. And in the park she tripped and I grabbed her and somehow we ended up on the ground.'

'Oh and you just lay there all helpless, is that it? Are you that weak?'

James stood up and paced back and forth across the room. A tiny patch of pink blotched each cheek. That was a sure sign he was annoyed … or guilty.

'Weak? If I was weak I would have slept with her when she invited herself around here last weekend while you were in Noosa.'

Helene jerked her head up at this unexpected news, pulling the stitches and triggering needles of pain.

'She came around here? And you let her in?'

'She wanted to watch the rugby.'

'She hates rugby.'

'She looked as if she was enjoying it to me, which is more than I can say for you. You never watch it with me.'

She put a hand to her ricocheting head, trying to soothe the pain.

'It's all you ever do – watch rugby. You may as well be married to it. You spend far more time with rugby than me. We do nothing fun anymore.'

'Well it's hard to have fun with someone who's always criticising me.'

'I don't criticise you.'

He stopped pacing and stood with his hands on his hips, the spots on his cheeks now glowing red. 'So it's not criticism when you tell me how to run the business or that you save people and I only save pictures?'

'I was only trying to be helpful. And my work is important. I'm not just going to sit at home having babies.'

'Not much chance of that, is there?'

'What do you mean?'

'It's pretty hard to have babies without sex.'

She looked down at her bandaged ankle to avoid his challenging stare. It hadn't been that long, had it? Honestly, was that all men ever thought about?

'So Nicolette offers herself to you on a rosy platter and you decide you may as well since you're getting none at home. Is that it?'

'No, I told you, nothing happened. It's you I want but you make it damn hard. I'm busting my guts to make a go of this business but you're too caught up with your own life to give me any support. Nicolette likes my work. She understands it. And to be honest when someone like her throws herself at you it's tempting.'

Helene felt as though she had been slapped. How could she have been so naïve? Nicolette had encouraged her to find someone else simply to get her out of the way so she could get her claws into James. Well if she wanted a fight, she would get one.

James continued. 'Anyway this isn't about Nicolette; it's about us. I decided not to do that work for her. I told her this morning. At least I've still got Bob's contract, when he gets around to signing it.'

'You told her this morning? Did you meet up with her?' She felt sick at the thought.

'I phoned her. That was difficult enough. I don't like to let people down.'

'Well it's her fault, the conniving cow. She had it all planned.'

'Had what all planned? Does this have something to do with why you were out last night?'

What should she say? Did he really need to know about Steve? She shifted uncomfortably. All this sitting on her bed was giving her a stiff back and a numb bum. No wonder immobile patients developed bed sores.

'I had a late meeting with Russell. He's offered me his job. He's moving to Sydney.' It was half the truth. James looked far from impressed.

'Nicolette seemed pretty confident you would be out late. How would she know about your meeting? Why would you tell her and not me?'

He sat on the end of the bed and studied her in silence. This was worse than being in court.

'I thought you would be excited about my new job. You don't seem very impressed.'

James started pacing the room again, clenching and unclenching his fists.

'Yes, I'm impressed but it doesn't add up. I've been straight with you but I get the feeling you're not being straight with me. What's going on?'

Tears filled her eyes. 'I am being straight. Why are you accusing me? I'm not the one who was being unfaithful.' A picture of her and Steve kissing under the pandanus palm barged into her mind.

'So much has happened – last night, the accident – I just need time to sort myself out.'

She couldn't bear to tell him everything right now. It was all such a mess. Her head throbbed with anger, embarrassment and guilt, not to mention the stitches.

26

The tentative truce lasted all weekend. James spent most of it out cycling, so he said. He could have been with Nicolette for all she knew, but her gut instinct was that he really was telling the truth – which, she had to admit, was more than she was doing.

The phone calls came on Monday.

'Helene, darling, how are you? I heard you had a car accident.' Her voice dripped with fake concern.

'What do you want, Nicolette?' The last thing she needed was a call from that scheming tart.

'Is that how you speak to your friend, especially after all I've done for you?'

'Done for me? What have you done for me except try to steal my husband?'

'Darling,' she purred. 'If it wasn't for me you would still be drifting along in your boring marriage. Like I said, there's nothing like a bit of competition to make you both appreciate what you've got. You should be thanking me.'

'I thought you were my friend. I can't believe you betrayed me like this.'

'The only person who's been betrayed is me. Barb and I were relying on James doing that work for us this week. He's let us down.'

'Well if you hadn't been so keen to get your claws into him, he might have done it.'

'So have you told him about your little rendezvous with Steve or should I? I'm sure he would like to know how you spent your weekend, and the other night.'

'It's none of your business. Just leave us alone.'

'Come on, Helene. It was just a bit of fun, and you weren't interested.'

'Not interested! He's my husband!'

'But aren't you more interested in Steve? Wasn't that the whole idea? To find someone more exciting?'

'It's fine for you to flit from man to man but James and I are married. We don't just run off with someone else the moment things get tough.'

'Really? I thought that was exactly what you were doing.'

'Well I'm not. It's all over with Steve – not that anything happened. And it had better be all over with you and James.'

'Sweetie, there's nothing to get over, apart from it being the first time I've had a man say no. You can have your husband. He might be good looking but he's way too straight for me.'

She dropped the phone and put her head in her hands. Why had she listened to Nicolette? How could Nicolette possibly think that making a play for James was helpful? The only other person she knew who would think like that was Steve. Her head pounded behind the scratchy stitches. What she needed was a good, strong cup of tea. She swung her legs off the bed and lowered her puffy, purple foot into the moon boot, tightening the velcro straps. The kitchen bench was littered with James' hastily eaten breakfast. While the jug boiled she tidied up, returning the room temperature milk to the fridge and the opened cereal and coffee packs to the pantry. She had just hobbled back to the bedroom, carefully trying not to slosh the brimming mug of tea, when the next phone call came.

'Hey, Helene. How's my best doctor doing? Mel's just told me the bad news. I was on the golf course with clients all day Friday. Lloyd sent his regards. I think he has a thing for you. Anyway what's the verdict? I heard the car was a write-off. How about you? Are you okay?'

She pulled her scattered emotions together and put on her work voice.

'Improving every day thanks to my two best friends: Voltarin and Panadol. The stitches should be able to come out by the end of the week.'

'Do you want me to send one of the nurses around to do it?'

'That would be great. It's not so easy when it's your own head.'

Russell laughed. 'You sound as though your head is in pretty good shape.' He cleared his throat. 'I know it's probably been the last thing on your mind but have you thought about the job? Sydney just phoned to see where we were at with a decision. No pressure, but when do you think you'll be back on board?'

'I'll be back next week. About the job: I haven't had a chance to talk to James yet, what with the accident and all.'

'Sure, sure, no problem. Speaking of James, I overheard an interesting conversation on Saturday night at the business awards. Great function – fantastic food and they kept the alcohol flowing. I think we might have picked up a few clients too.'

'So what was the conversation?'

'I only caught part of it but it didn't sound good. This blond woman – a real stunner – sounded as though she was bad-mouthing James. It was only when they mentioned graphic designers that I made the connection. She said something about him not being reliable, how she would never use him. I may have misheard. There was a lot of noise.'

Helene's mind raced. It had to be Nicolette. Of course she would be at the business awards on the prowl for her next conquest. But would she spread such lies about James? He was totally reliable; it was something he prided himself on. She slumped back on the pillows and closed her eyes trying to shut out visions of Nicolette with James right here in this house, perhaps on this bed. Nicolette kissing James at the wine bar, Nicolette on top of James in the park and Nicolette slandering James to some smitten bloke at the business awards. How could she? Her cup of tea was cold by the time she reached to take a sip. Her head was spinning and her forehead throbbed.

The mobile rang again. It was James.

'I had to call you.' He sounded flat, drained, hopeless. 'Bob's put a hold on the contract.'

'What? You mean the one you've been waiting for, the one that we need? Why?'

'He said that a colleague had recommended another designer. I've heard of him – he's been around for ages and he's good. So Bob wants to give him a go before he commits to either of us.'

'That's so unfair. What did you say?'

'What could I say?' His voice wobbled.

'I don't know. You could have …' She stopped herself. A lecture wouldn't help. 'I'm really sorry.' She was surprised at how much she truly meant it.

'I don't understand why he suddenly changed his mind. He's seen my work and he likes it. He'd already picked me over the other two designers. I just don't get it.'

Her heart dropped as the pieces clicked into place. 'I know exactly who's to blame for this.'

27

It was mid-afternoon when a taxi pulled up outside. Mere was back. Helene watched her trundle her overnight bag down the driveway to the guest house, stopping every so often to cough. She'd had that cough when she arrived, but it seemed worse. She must ask her about it. It wasn't long before she heard Mere come in through the back balcony door.

'Hello?' she called as she walked through the house and tapped on the bedroom door.

'Come in, Mere. How was the weekend?'

'Wonderful. We had so much to catch up on after all these years. Shirley hasn't changed a bit. She's still as busy as ever with her charities and church. But what about you, my dear, are you on the mend?'

It wasn't what she said so much as how she said it that breached Helene's wall of composure. Tears rushed to her eyes and spilled down her cheeks before she could stop them. She could keep up her self-sufficient face with her mum and James, but not with Mere. There was something about her that stripped all that away.

She wiped away the tears and sniffed. 'I'm sorry. I don't know what's come over me. I'll be all right in a minute.'

'I have all the time in the world, dearie.'

Just like the tears, the words tumbled out, telling Mere the whole story from the chat with Nicolette in the café to James' phone call this morning.

Mere sat on the edge of the bed, saying nothing until Helene had finished. She leaned over and took Helene's hand.

'Don't fret, my dear. All is not lost.'

Helene stifled a sob.

'I just don't know. I haven't even told James about Steve yet. I don't know if I can or even if I should.'

'A marriage doesn't work too well without truth, even if it hurts. I think it would be best to tell James what happened but reassure him that you love him.'

'But that's just it. I don't think I do. I didn't feel in love with him before all this started. That's partly why I listened to Nicolette's advice. And when I think about what she and he have been up to I have even less feelings for him. I think it might be over.'

'Feelings.' Mere spoke the word as though she was stamping on a cockroach. 'They are about as reliable in a marriage as a weather vane in Wellington – all over the place.' She patted Helene's hand. 'Love isn't a noun, it's a verb. It's about doing and saying kind things, despite your feelings. The feelings come after the actions, not before.'

'But I'm so angry at him and Nicolette ... and myself. How could I have been so stupid?'

'You're not the first and you're not the last. I too have been angry at others and myself. That's why I am writing this book; so my children and grandchildren know about the hurt and injustice that the New Zealand government caused to our people, but more importantly to learn how to move forward. Whether it's a person or a government, the same principles apply.'

'I have no idea how to move forward. It's all such a mess.'

Mere patted her hand. 'Let me tell you a little of my story. It might help.'

Helene nodded. 'I'd like that.' She certainly wasn't going anywhere and it would be a relief to not have to think about her own problems for a while.

Mere stood up. 'But first we need a nice cup of tea and some of my biscuits to cheer us up.'

'If you insist!' Helene already felt brighter.

Mere arrived back with two cups of tea delicately balanced on matching saucers and a plate laden with choc-chip cookies – enough to feed ten people, not two. 'Just in case we get hungry,' she laughed. She handed Helene a cup of tea and placed the biscuits between them on the bed.

The tea was hot and strong. Helene reached for a biscuit. She needed some comfort food.

'So tell me about your book.'

Mere coughed and cleared her throat. 'It's about forgiveness … such a difficult thing. People hurt you; governments hurt you. They stole from my people – changed the rules to suit themselves until they had just about taken all of our land. By the 1970s all we had left was Takaparawhau. Most people know it as Bastion Point. But I should really start at the beginning.'

She finished off her biscuit, washing it down with her tea.

'Before the Pakeha came to Auckland – when the government was still up in Russell – my tribe, Ngati Whatua, owned thousands of hectares of land; pretty much the whole of Auckland. Harbours, wetlands, streams, hills, lush bush and beaches, everything we needed to live. We were a powerful tribe. Rich and powerful. But we also had enemies, so our chief invited Governor Hobson to move the capital to Auckland. It would give us protection as well as access to education, medicine and trade. We sold him twelve hundred hectares for just three hundred and forty one pounds to set up a settlement.

'Over the next ten years we sold other blocks of land for ridiculously cheap prices until by 1850 we had only a fraction of our land left – about seven hundred acres at Orakei. Our chiefs fought to keep our land communal so we couldn't lose any more, but in 1898 the government went against their requests and changed the law to individual ownership. They knew some of our people would sell their land for bargain prices, and they did. Two years later, the government built a sewage pipe right across our bay – Okahu Bay – right where we swam and fished. It didn't stop us fishing but it did make us sick.

The hospital used to flush all sorts of things down the drain and some ended up floating in our bay – amputated limbs, dead foetuses. It was disgusting. Many of our young kids got typhoid and died from swimming in that putrid water. My brother died when he was thirteen.'

She stopped for a moment, her eyes unfocussed, as if staring back in time. When she spoke her voice was quiet and grief shone in her eyes.

'You never forget a tragedy like that. He was my only brother and he was bright. Mum said he would be a doctor when he grew up. He talked and laughed all the time. He was a really good swimmer and he always caught us lots of fish to eat.'

'I'm so sorry. That's terrible. How could they do that?' She could hardly believe it was true. Surely a hospital wouldn't flush foetuses down the drain?

'They refused to connect us to the city's fresh water supply. They were trying to move us off the last vestige of our land. Thirty or so years later they built Tamaki Drive so all the people who lived further around at Kohimarama and St Heliers could get into the city. The only problem was that they had to drive past us to get there. The final straw came when Queen Elizabeth was scheduled to visit at Christmas 1953. The government was determined to "tidy up the mess". To get public sympathy, the government said we were living in squalor and needed new houses. What a load of rubbish! Some of those homes had been built for engineers and contractors when they built Tamaki Drive. They had verandas and every modern amenity. Anyway, they built twenty-seven houses up the hill, near to the three they had built earlier. Thirty houses for fifty or sixty families.

'But that's not enough!'

'Exactly.' She continued. 'Some wanted to move but most realised what was going on and were dead against it. Especially the kuia, the old women. I still remember the wailing as the men carried them from their burning whares. They would have stubbornly stayed and burned to death otherwise. As it was, we dug graves for six weeks. Within a year they had all died. It broke their spirit, their wairua.'

She took a sip of her tea and a determined breath before continuing.

'So we were booted up the hill. And so much for the promise that we could rent to buy. Six years later when the men took their rent books in to buy the houses, they were told the policy had changed and they could no longer buy their homes. So we went from being self-sufficient to dependent and in debt. That's why, in 1978 when the government tried to take the last of our land to subdivide it for more fancy houses, we stood and fought. I still remember word for word what our leader said at that first meeting as he urged us to take a stand: *What have we got to lose? All we have left is a quarter acre graveyard, and that is full to overflowing. The pakeha have taken all our land so if we haven't got anything, we can't lose anything. But if we succeed many people would have much to gain.*

'We camped on that land for five hundred and six days and we won. It was big news. People all over New Zealand and the world supported us – Pakeha, Maori, even a few of you Aussies! Of course there were plenty against us too. But God was on our side. Even when the army and police dragged us off our land and arrested two hundred and twenty-two of us, it all turned to good. People were shocked that this could happen in good old New Zealand. Only thirty cases were heard before the public outcry made them drop the rest of the charges. But the wounds go deep in my people. One precious little girl died up at that camp, in another fire. What a price to pay for our land. We cried for months ...'

Mere put her cup of tea on the floor. 'Excuse me, I'm just going to the bathroom.'

She returned a few minutes later, her eyes slightly bloodshot. 'There's nothing like a good cry while you're sitting on the loo.'

Her smile seemed to permeate her whole body, filling it with warmth. How could she look so calm, almost happy, after telling such a tragic story?

'Everyone gets hurt by other people. Some worse than others. What matters is what you do with that hurt.'

143

'What can you do?' asked Helene. 'We're just victims of someone else's selfish, mean behaviour. They ruin our lives and we can't do a thing about it.' A series of snapshots flicked through her mind: her dad swigging from his hip flask, the man from the bank apologising as he locked them out of their home, scratching her flea bitten legs while her mother trawled her hair for nits in a dingy bed-sit. She shook away the memories. This was about James and Nicolette, not her father.

Mere continued. 'I used to think that but I've learned different. Even though we can't control what people do to us, we still have control over what we do about it. And the best thing to do is forgive.'

'Forgive? That's like letting them get away with it. They should pay for what they've done.'

'That's not for us to decide. There's a saying that unforgiveness is like drinking poison and hoping the other person dies. I've seen too many of my people eaten up with bitterness and anger. It ate at their insides – made them sick – and spilled out to the people around them, wrecking their lives too. Unforgiveness. It's a terrible thing.'

'I can forgive James. After all, if I'm honest with myself, I've behaved just as badly. But Nicolette's a different story. She's ruined James' reputation and she's not the slightest bit sorry. She thinks she's done us a favour. I can't forgive her.'

'No one can,' replied Mere.

'What do you mean? You just said that I need to forgive and now you say that I can't do it even if I wanted to?' Helene was confused.

Mere munched on a biscuit for a few moments before answering. 'I tried it. Again and again I would resolve to forgive those people for what they had stolen from my people, the pain, the needless deaths, the injustice. It would work for a while but then I'd be haunted by memories – my brother gasping for breath on his bed as the typhoid took him; finding Dad most Saturday nights, drunk and sobbing over Rewiti's grave; my grandmother curled up in her bed like a bundle of sticks, refusing to eat and drink because they had burned down her home. All the pain and anger would come flooding back. I could not forgive. Eventually I asked God for help. I told him how I wanted to forgive but I couldn't. I was sick of the sleepless nights, the nightmares when I did manage to sleep and the arthritis creeping into my fingers.'

Helene placed her tea cup on a pile of medical journals sitting on her bedside table. 'Are you saying that your bitterness caused your arthritis? It was more likely psychosomatic or just a coincidence.

'All I know is that when I asked the Lord to help me forgive the government, the officials and all the people who had hurt me, I felt a huge weight lift off and I have never had a hint of arthritis since.'

'I'm not sure I believe in God.'

Mere smiled her warm smile. 'That's okay.'

The question tumbled from her lips before her logic could shut it down. 'Would you talk to him for me?' What was she doing, asking Mere to pray to someone she wasn't even sure existed? And yet, why not? If she was going to ask any higher power, God would have to be a better bet than Nicolette's universe. Look what trouble it had caused her.

'I have been talking to him about you and James ever since I arrived here.'

'Really? But you hardly know us.'

'You don't need to send him orders you know. He's not a restaurant. He's well aware of the situation.' She patted Helene on the hand and grinned. 'And now how about I peel a few potatoes and bless you and James with a good old fashioned Kiwi dinner?'

'You don't have to do that, Mere. James can pick up takeaways on the way home.'

'If he's anything like his parents I'm sure he'd prefer a roast. I have a lovely piece of pork sitting in my fridge ready to cook. It's too big for me to eat on my own. I'll just go and pop it in the oven. I'll bring it over when it's ready. Are you sure you have everything you need?' She started to cough and quickly pulled out a wad of tissues from her pocket to hold over her mouth.

'I'm fine, thanks Mere. But you need to look after yourself. How long have you had that cough?'

'It's nothing. Just a bit of a wheeze. I've always had a touchy chest. Don't you worry about me, sweetie. I'm perfectly alright.'

She gathered up the empty tea cups and plate. 'Now you have a nice rest and I'll pop over a bit later.'

Helene could hear her coughing again as she walked across the back lawn to the guest house. It didn't sound good.

28

It was one of the most humiliating things she had had to do. Being the victim had given her a sense of righteous power. Now, on Mere's advice and for her own peace of mind, she had to relinquish it. It was hard. Her heart thumped as she told James all about Steve, the weekend at Noosa and the arranged meeting at the hotel. His face was a map of emotions. His eyes opened wide as she started the story, then dropped to the floor, then finally stared dully back at her. His mouth set in a hard line and the tell-tale tiny, red patches spotted his cheeks. He was silent, but by the way he was chewing his lip, she could tell he was stewing over her guilty admission. She waited.

Finally he spoke. 'So you didn't sleep with him.'

'No.'

'But you wanted to.'

'No.' It wasn't convincing enough to fool him.

He rolled his eyes and started to pace the room. 'Be honest, Helene. If you'd had the chance you would have, wouldn't you?'

'Just as you would have with Nicolette.'

James turned on her, his voice raised in anger. 'She's not my ex-girlfriend. There's no history between us and there never will be. Don't make out that I'm the guilty one. I didn't hook up with some old flame for the weekend.'

He looked as though she had stabbed him in the back and it suddenly hit her that she hadn't thought about how he would feel. Tears pricked her eyes yet again. But this time the tears weren't for her, they were for James.

147

'It wasn't like that. I accidentally met him, we went out to dinner, but nothing happened.'

'So why did you arrange to meet him again here in Brisbane? Where did you think that would lead to?' His eyes flashed.

She squirmed on her bed. Tell the truth, Mere had said.

'At first I thought it would be exciting but, as I told you, I realised what a stupid idea it was and I didn't go.'

She fumbled for some tissues and blew her nose through the tears that trickled down her cheeks.

'So you would risk our marriage just for some excitement? Grow up, Helene. You're starting to sound just like Nicolette.' James glared at her across the room. A clatter in the kitchen, followed by Mere coughing, interrupted their argument.

'Mere's cooked us a roast. She must have brought it over.'

James marched out the door, clearly relieved by the change of subject. 'I'll see if she wants to eat with us. It's the least we can do to thank her for all her help around here.'

'I'll come out soon,' she mumbled but he had already gone.

She wasn't sure what made her do it. It had been years since she had opened the dusty shoebox shoved at the back of the wardrobe. She wiped off the sticky remains of a spider web and lifted the lid. Inside lay the letters from her father, unopened and yellowed. She had vowed never to read them, never to speak to him, and definitely never to marry anyone like him. She touched the top envelope tentatively, as though it might reach out and bite. One enormous tear dropped onto the envelope and spread out just as the pool water had over the pavers on that terrible day. Her finger absently stroked the wet patch. Perhaps one day soon she would read them.

***

By the time she'd splashed her tear-streaked face and limped out to the kitchen Mere and James had set the table and served the dinner. Three plates laden with thickly sliced roast pork, crackling, roast vegetables, gravy and apple sauce sat on three placemats and a bottle of white wine stood ready to be poured. James and Mere talked through second helpings of roast meat and a moist lemon pudding that Mere had also made. Helene could barely get through her small serving. She sat quietly pushing the food around her plate. James asked Mere about her childhood growing up with his mum which naturally led to the story she had told Helene earlier that day. She didn't mind hearing it again. It was fascinating, yet tragic, and it stirred something in her that she couldn't quite identify.

Later that night she lay on her side of the bed, unable to sleep. James lay asleep on his stomach, his head resting on his muscular arms. At least he wasn't too angry to sleep in the same bed, although he was so far over his side that his feet hung off the edge. She had never seen him so angry. Would he believe that nothing had happened between her and Steve? She had come so close to falling, again, for Steve's dubious charms. Thank goodness she hadn't gone to the hotel. Had it really been just good luck that she'd spotted herself in that mirror? And the sudden headache in Noosa; was that also a mere coincidence or did it have something to do with Mere's prayers? Her mind raced round and round. Now James had lost the business he was relying on. How would they pay the mortgage on the business and this house? The higher salary that Russell was offering her wouldn't be enough. And did she really want less patient time? Apart from the management side, this new job, with its endless socialising, seemed little more than glorified public relations. She was bound to bump into Nicolette at some function or other. That was the last thing she needed. It seemed that the part of her work that she liked the most was the part she would have no time for. She thought of her granddad: his easy grin as he held a little Aboriginal girl or reassured an anxious mother. No cocktail evenings or marketing strategies for him.

James rolled over, turning his bare back towards her. With each breath his trapezius and deltoid muscles rippled subtly. She touched him gently, the way she used to when they were first married, then curled onto her side, careful not to squash the stitches in her head.

29

James was pensive and distant the next morning. He left for work early, giving her a peck on the cheek that felt more obligatory than meaningful. She could hardly expect more considering the news she had dumped on him yesterday. She was still brooding when Mere trudged up the steps onto the back veranda. She was breathing heavily as though she had just walked up four flights of stairs, not four steps.

'Phew, those steps get steeper every day.' She plonked into a chair opposite where Helene lay stretched out in the lounge and wiped her brow. 'It's nice to see you up. Would you like a cup of tea?'

Helene smiled. 'Not just yet, thanks Mere. I need to pace myself. I don't think I've ever drunk so much tea as with you these past few days.'

'A lot of problems have been solved over a cup of tea, you know. Have you heard the saying: The sixth cup of tea between friends is the best.'

'Six cups? Who can spare that amount of time, or handle that amount of caffeine!'

Mere laughed which turned into a deep hacking cough. She reached into her pocket for some tissues and held them to her mouth. As she pulled them away Helene caught a glimpse of red. Was that blood?

'How long have you been coughing like that?'

Mere had brushed off the question yesterday but this time she hesitated, her expression becoming more serious. 'Actually, it's been over a year. I try to ignore it but I have to admit it's been getting worse.'

'So you haven't seen a doctor about it?'

'I don't like to go to doctors unless I absolutely have to. I grew up with a mistrust of doctors. Old habits die hard, even if you know better.'

'You really should have a chest x-ray to rule out anything serious. It may be something quite simple that I can give you some medication for. Will you let me arrange it for you please?'

'Don't bother yourself about me, dearie. I can organise one next week when I get back to New Zealand.'

'But will you?' Coughing blood was a serious sign that needed immediate investigation. 'Promise me you'll do it as soon as you get back.'

Mere opened her hand and studied the speckled red contents. 'It's the first time I've seen blood. I suppose I do need to find out.' She sat quietly for a moment, a sombre expression on her face, and then looked up at Helene with her bright smile. 'Now I really do need that cup of tea. What about you?'

'All right, but only to keep you company.'

***

'There's something I want to give you.'

Mere handed Helene a small parcel of pale green tissue paper tied with a ribbon. They sat on the balcony, a pot of tea between them on the wooden table. The early morning sun framed Mere's head in a halo of light. Helene wrapped her hands around the mug of tea and took her first sip of caffeine for the day. It wasn't yet six in the morning but James was already out running. He would be back soon to take Mere to the airport. Birds hopped across the back garden, pecking at worms and flitting noisily through the neighbour's mock orange hedge. The air was still and crisp. An inquisitive kookaburra swooped down and landed on Mere's suitcase, which stood waiting on the driveway in front of the guest house. Finding nothing of interest, it flew up to a nearby gum tree and chattered out its sleep-shattering laugh. Perhaps it too, was saying goodbye.

'What is it?' Helene pressed the paper.

151

'Something that I hope will help you as much as it has helped me.'

She delicately tugged the ribbon and opened the tissue paper. Inside rested Mere's pendent.

She held the smooth stone in her palm, tilting it so the sunlight illuminated its deep green hues. Its smooth weight felt good to hold, almost soothing.

'I can't take this, Mere. It's yours! Surely it's special to you?'

'Yes, it is special. Greenstone is a special type of jade found only in the South Island of New Zealand. We call it pounamu. My grandfather carved this one many years ago and passed it on to my father. He planned to give it to Rewiti but when he died …'

Her voice faltered.

'Then surely it should go to one of your children rather than me?'

Mere shook her head. 'I had always thought that would be the case but I think it's meant for you.'

'Why me?'

'It's just a strong impression that I should give it to you, and the more I prayed about it, the stronger the conviction became.'

'But I don't deserve it.'

'You don't need to deserve a gift; you just receive it. And then say thank you.' Her amused scolding lightened the moment.

'Thank you, Mere. This is so special. I will wear it always.' She hung it around her neck. The stone felt cool against her chest. She rubbed its smooth surface.

'My grandfather named this stone Rongo, which means peace. I used to think the stone gave me peace but I finally realised that it wasn't the stone but the maker of the stone.'

'You mean your grandfather?'

'I mean the maker of all stones, trees, people, the universe. God is the one who gives us peace.'

'Does the shape have any special meaning?' she asked, trying to change the subject.

'The fishing hook is often given to people who are going on a journey. It's travelled with me on my journey through life. Hopefully you will keep it with you wherever your journey takes you.'

Helene touched the stone again and sighed.

'I don't know where I'm going at the moment ...'

Mere placed her warm hand on Helene's.

'You and James will be fine. I am sure of that. As for the rest ... you will know deep in your heart what feels right. Your heart may tell you something different from your intellect and logic but I've found it's usually right.'

'Are you all ready to go, Mere?'

James stepped out onto the balcony, rubbing his hands through his damp hair. His face was ruddy but he looked cool in a casual v-necked shirt that she hadn't seen before. Isn't that what men did when they were having an affair? Her dad had done exactly that – swapping his old, scuffed shoes for smart Italian ones and spending a fortune on new suits and frequent haircuts. It was a dead giveaway. Or had Nicolette bought it for him? This was ridiculous; she had to get a grip on her imagination. But it was too late. She was already angry at the possibility.

Mere stood up and gave Helene a big hug.

'Goodbye my dear and thank you. It has been a wonderful, restful and productive time for me.'

'Thank you, Mere, – for everything. Take care and please get that cough checked out as soon as possible.'

'I will.' She made her way down the steps and over to the car. James slammed the boot shut and turned to Helene as he opened the car door.

'See you tonight.'

He didn't even kiss her, which was another bad sign. She waved as the car backed out of the driveway, then put her hand to her chest, over the soothing green stone.

30

Three weeks later Helene was saying goodbye again. Tears streamed down her face as she watched the plane taxi down the runway and take off into the cloudless sky.

'Don't worry. I'm sure you'll see him again soon,' consoled the woman next to her as she waved at the departing plane. Helene forced a smile but the tears kept coming. She wasn't so sure.

James had dumped the news on her just as she had arrived home from the gym late one night. He was sitting at the table tucking into a carton of takeaway noodles.

'My old boss called me today,' he said through a mouthful. He had taken to buying his own dinner despite Helene's efforts to cook his favourite meals. Her heart slumped every time he walked in with a paper bag of food.

'What did he want?'

'He offered me a job.'

'You wouldn't want to go back there would you?'

'It's a three month contract managing one of their offices. He's offering big money and there's a possibility I could stay on.'

'What about your own business? I thought you wanted to be independent.'

James looked at her, his face as hard as steel. 'Your friend stuffed that up for me. My name is mud.'

Helene was about to retort that Nicolette was no friend of hers but forced herself to keep quiet. This wasn't about Nicolette. 'So there's no hope for your business?'

He sighed and put his head in his hands. 'I'm already overdue with the rent and the landlord isn't the forgiving type. If I don't come up with the money by the end of the week, I'm out. And I can't see any clients wanting to take me on right now.'

'Can we borrow against the house?'

'I phoned them today. They won't lend us any more and with interest rates the way they are we couldn't afford the repayments anyway.'

Helene poured herself a glass of water and sat down. 'So where is this office they want you to manage?'

He scooped up another forkful of noodles. 'New Zealand.'

Now he was gone, just a black smudge in the sky. Wiping away her tears, she turned and walked through the huddles of embracing couples and cheery families, out into the glare of the midday sun. She walked across the car park and unlocked her car. As she tossed her bag on the empty passenger seat she saw James' jumper still lying on the floor. She picked it up and held it to her face. Her memory rewound to a little girl scrunched in her bed, sobbing into her father's jumper and hoping he would come home. The tears started to flow again. She tried to reason with herself. This was different. James would return. It was only three months. *You tore your house down with your own hands. He's not coming back.* The thought was loud and insistent. She felt ill. She wrapped her arms around herself and dropped her head on the steering wheel. The sun beat down on her through the glass gradually turning the car into a sauna. Eventually she turned the key, switched on the air conditioning and drove home. Alone.

31

Helene dug her fingers into the glass lolly jar, searching for white jelly beans. There were none left. She plonked it back on her desk next to a pile of business management textbooks that Russell had lent her. Picking up a pen she doodled on her prescription pad. That was about all it was good for these days. She glanced at the *Principles of Health Economics* textbook which lay open in front of her, the words blurring before her. She rubbed her eyes and tried to focus. Finance was not her forte and yet, if she was to take over from Russell, she needed to get a grasp of at least the basics.

'Give me anatomy and physiology any day,' she muttered.

'Hey, did I just hear you talking to yourself?' Russell stood at the door, grinning. 'Surely the study isn't getting to you, is it? I thought you'd be used to it.' He strolled in and settled on the red leather couch, plonking his patent leather shoes on the coffee table.

Helene swivelled her chair around to face him.

'It's fine. I'm just a bit tired, that's all.'

'You'll get used to it. My first few months I was dead beat all the time. But it looks as though you'll have plenty of time to acclimatise to the job: Sydney just called.'

'Surely not another delay?'

Russell sighed.

'Do I look happy? This time it's "internal issues".' He raised his hands in visual quotation marks. 'They're holding off on the job until the new year.'

She didn't know whether to feel relieved or disappointed.

'Well if we have another few months to hand over perhaps I can see a few more patients.' She picked up her stethoscope and pretended to dust it off.

'Don't get me wrong, Russell, I'm looking forward to the new job, but we did agree that I could continue some clinical work.' She waved the stethoscope around. 'I don't want to forget how to use this.'

'Sure, sure. We'll schedule you in for a few more sessions.' He rubbed his hands through his salt and peppered hair, messing it up as though he'd just dried off after a surfing session.

'I could do with a cold beer right now.'

Helene moved to sit opposite him. As she stood up, her vision blurred again. Postural hypotension – she needed a drink herself. She reached for her water bottle and looked at her watch.

'It's not long until we need to be at the stadium, is it? I'm sure they'll have the fridge stocked just for you,' she teased.

'And for Lloyd. He likes the odd drink.'

Helene unscrewed her water bottle and finished off the contents. Her empty stomach recoiled at the sudden assault. 'So what's the agenda tonight? Purely social?'

'Absolutely social, although …' He grinned just the way James used to when he would assure her that they didn't have much farther to go on those marathon bush walks he loved to take her on. Her heart slumped at the memory. 'Although you want me to guide the conversation in some way, right?'

'Hey, all I know is that Lloyd likes you. He's worried that our new whole health program will turn his staff into a bunch of alternative health nuts. Just reassure him that it's not all yoghurt, yoga and yin yang.'

She didn't have a problem with the concept. Her own patient observations, and more recently Mere's stories, lined up with the burgeoning scientific publications on the 'whole health' theory. She touched her greenstone pendant. But what would Mere have to say about the group they had contracted to implement the 'be happy, stay healthy' program? She remembered their chat about the universe. It reminded her of Nicolette, which only added to the pain in her stomach.

'I think he would be happier if we could get someone more medically trained to run the seminars. He told me he didn't want any "psycho mumbo jumbo", to use his words.'

'This group came highly recommended.'

'Yes, but we are a medical practice. There are already too many patients who take more notice of their naturopath than us. Ask any of the other doctors here. They all struggle with it.'

Russell held up his hands in surrender.

'Okay, okay. If it will keep clients like Lloyd happy – and you doctors – I'll look into it. Now about next week, are you fine to attend that dinner on Thursday and the conference down the coast on the weekend?'

She mentally flicked through her diary, brimming with dinners, functions and meetings. Since taking on this new job she had hardly more than two nights in a row at home which was a blessing in some ways. Without James, it felt more like an empty shell than a home.

'I'm looking forward to it,' she replied.

'It's a shame that James isn't here for the game tonight. It should be a good one. But he'll get to see plenty with you once he's back in the real world. How much longer is he stuck in New Zealand?'

'I'm not sure.'

It was the truth. The few times they spoke he sounded so happy that she wondered if he would come back at all. Was it just the job or had he found some Kiwi woman to keep him warm at night? Theirs wasn't an official separation but it might as well have been. Sometimes it hit her during the shallow social banter of a cocktail party, other times it was when she arrived home after an evening of flitting from one potential client to the next. Her footsteps echoed through the dark, empty house and the cold bed engulfed her in loneliness. She rubbed Mere's greenstone pendent and pasted on a smile.

Russell stood up. 'We'd better get going. I'll call a taxi and meet you downstairs in ten minutes, okay?'

Helene stuffed two business management textbooks into her briefcase. She was just touching up her make-up when her mobile went. Fumbling around in her handbag, she found it just before it cut to voice mail.

'Helene speaking.'

She walked towards the glass windows and stared out at the city below.

'Hi, it's me.'

A thrill of hope ran through her. James usually e-mailed and his infrequent calls were always at home. Perhaps he really was missing her, perhaps he did still care.

'Hi darling. How are you?'

'I'm fine.' He didn't sound fine. He sounded sort of upset.

'What's the matter? Is something wrong?' What could it be? He'd lost his job, he'd found someone else, he wanted a divorce?

'It's bad news, I'm afraid. It's Mere. She's dead.'

32

Helene spotted James as soon as she and Shirley exited immigration. He stood to one side, his hands in the pockets of his leather jacket. He raised a hand in greeting and wandered towards them, a relaxed smile on his face. Helene's heart fluttered. He seemed happy to see her, or was it just a show for his mother.

'Hi, Mum. It's good to see you.'

Shirley flung her arms around him and kissed him on the cheek, then held him at arm's length and studied him. 'I think you've lost weight. I hope you are eating properly.'

'I'm fine, Mum,' he laughed. He turned to Helene, wrapping his arms around her and kissing her on the lips. 'I missed you,' he whispered in her ear. She breathed a silent sigh of relief.

'I missed you too.'

Pushing their luggage trolley James led the way towards the airport car park. As they stepped out into the dark evening a blast of cold air hit them. Shirley, who had been chattering away to James stopped mid-sentence.

'My goodness, I'd forgotten how cold that wind can be!'

Before either of them could comment James' phone started ringing. He fished it from his jeans pocket and turned away to answer it.

'James here.'

Helene could hear a faint female voice. He laughed and stepped a little further away. 'Sure, that should be fine. See you then.' He shoved the phone back in his jeans and smiled at the two of them.

'Work,' he explained. 'Let's get home. It's freezing out here.'

Helene couldn't help herself. All the way to James' apartment her mind churned. Was the girl on the phone really 'work'? Why was she calling so late at night? Could he be having a fling with one of his staff? Could Nicolette have pursued him over here?

***

It was well after midnight when they finally collapsed into bed. Their room was a loft above the main living area where Shirley was fluffing around, traipsing from the sofa bed to the bathroom and back. James pulled her to him and began kissing her but their every move brought a series of groans and squeaks from the bed. He pulled away. 'We can't do this with Mum hearing everything,' he whispered. 'We'll have to wait.' They snuggled up to sleep but Helene remained awake wondering if this was the first time he had shared his bed, and imagining the worst.

The next morning he dumped the bombshell.

'Guess what? The bloke I'm covering for has resigned; decided to stay in Europe. They've offered me the job permanently.' His face could have lit up the entire city.

'You mean live here in Auckland?'

'Why not? There's nothing for me back in Brisbane. The work's good, the money's great and it's a beautiful country. It would be like a fresh start.'

'What about my job? And our house?'

'I've thought about that. We could rent it out. Wasn't that nurse at your work – Judith, isn't it? – looking for something close to town? We could stay here in this apartment.'

He flung open the plantation shutters. They were right on the waterfront, the harbour still and grey under heavy rainclouds. Directly below them a line of luxury yachts lolled at their moorings, surrounded on three sides by scrubbed decking. A waiter puffing a cigarette lounged outside a sleepy cafe and a scattering of early morning joggers showed the first signs of the stirring city.

'It's a fantastic spot. You could pick up a job nearby and walk to work like I do.'

'What about my job in Brisbane? Do you expect me to just lay it down and leave?'

Her words wiped the smile from his face. He sighed and shoved his hands deep in his pockets. 'You don't have to decide right now. Just think about it, okay?'

It was all she could think about as she pulled on a navy designer dress and brushed her hair. Where was her ordered, predictable life? Right now it felt more like that terrifying, recurrent dream, that gut-wrenching helplessness as her raft plummeted over the waterfall. She applied mascara and a deep red lipstick. What would Mere say? What would she have done? She had only known her a few short weeks and yet she valued her advice more than anyone else. Now she was gone.

33

Helene wrapped her navy cardigan tightly around her in a vain attempt to ward off the damp cold of the morning. Her high heels sank into the sodden ground and the grass brushed wet against her bare ankles. She followed James and Shirley towards the crowd of mourners. There must have been at least one hundred people already gathered, looking as bleak as the grey clouds that rolled across the sky. Above the crowd, like little spots of incongruously happy colour, umbrellas sheltered the people from an incessant drizzle. James held his mum's elbow, supporting her gently. She hadn't cried at all on the flight over from Brisbane the night before, nor this morning in James' apartment as they dressed for the funeral. It was only as James pulled into the marae car park, manoeuvring past the mini vans and buses, that she had pulled a lacy handkerchief out of her handbag and started to dab her eyes. Most people would use tissues, but not Shirley. She liked the old traditional ways and somehow, in this country, on this hillside that seemed so rural despite being in the centre of the city, a handkerchief seemed so much more appropriate. Shirley stumbled on a clump of grass and James tightened his grasp on her arm to steady her.

'I'm fine, dear, don't fuss.'

She stopped and turned to Helene, with red eyes that belied her protestation of fineness.

'What about you, dear? Are you all right in that thin little dress? I should have told you to pack some warm clothes. The New Zealand spring is so unpredictable.'

'I will be okay. I'm sure I'll warm up once we're inside.'

James held his umbrella over the three of them.

'Don't worry, Mum. It's been like this all week. It will clear up later.'

He sounded like a local despite living here for only a few months. Helene looked at the crowd waiting in front of an ornately carved archway that led through to a paved area as large as two tennis courts. The design made it look like an enormous woven mat spread out before an imposing triangular building. Maori carvings sloped from the ground up each side to meet in the centre. The figures looked half human, with their shell eyes luminous against the black paint. Contrasting with the black was a deep red centre column carved with equally ferocious figures. They looked as though they were guarding the building. Mere was inside there – in a coffin. She couldn't believe it. A few short months ago she and Mere had been sitting on her veranda saying goodbye. She hadn't realised it would be forever. Helene felt numb – anaesthetised by shock. She wrapped her frozen fingers around the greenstone pendant, hugging both hands against her chest and hunching her shoulders to keep warm. She felt completely under-dressed and over-bright, even in navy. Everyone around her wore black. The men in dark suits or black shirts over black trousers, the women in long black skirts or trousers. She was the only one with bare legs except, thank goodness, for two young women in smart black suits and high heels. They looked so like Mere. She nudged Shirley. 'Do you think they could they be Mere's granddaughters?'

Shirley shook her head. 'They might be relatives but not her immediate family. They will already be in the meeting house. They would have been there for the past two days.'

'Two days?'

Shirley smiled. 'In the old days some went on for weeks or even months. The more mana or respect a person had, the longer their tangi. Now it's usually just three days.'

'Do they go home at night?' Three days for a funeral. That was more than long enough.

'The immediate family and close friends will have stayed with Mere day and night, never leaving her, always by her side. It's Maori custom.'

'You mean they actually sleep in the same room as the coffin?' James asked.

'Right next to it. I know it sounds morbid. I used to be terrified at the thought until Mere explained to me how comforting it is to have time to talk, to cry, to say the things you wished you had said when they were alive. She was always at tangis when we were kids. Half the class were.'

'What did the teachers think about that?'

'It was a normal part of growing up around here. They understood that a tangi took precedence over everything else, even school.'

'Excuse me. Are you Shirley?' The resonant voice emanated from a striking man who, from the looks of his solid shoulders and thighs, must have played rugby when he was younger. The first hints of grey streaked a thick wave of hair which he kept sweeping off his face with his hand.

Shirley looked startled. 'Yes, yes I'm Shirley. How did you know?'

'I'm Derek, Mere's youngest. Mum told me all about her wonderful visit with you in Australia. I'm so glad she got to see you before she ...'

His melodious voice faltered.

James put his hand out to shake Derek's, filling the grieving gap.

'Hey, mate. We're so sorry about your mum. It's such a shock. I'm James, Shirley's youngest. And this is my wife, Helene.'

'Ah, yes.' A warm smile spread across his face. 'She stayed with you in Brisbane, didn't she?'

Helene answered. 'She was wonderful, a real help to us, in many ways.' Her voice also trailed off stifled by a rush of memories: Mere gardening, Mere laughing, Mere talking, Mere crying, Mere coughing, Mere praying.

'Yeah, that's Mum.' He spoke as though she was still alive. 'Always helping. Aunty told me you were coming over. We really appreciate it. Thought I'd come out to say hello and explain what's happening. This is your first tangi, isn't it?'

Shirley furrowed her forehead in concentration. 'I vaguely remember coming here to Mere's grandmother's tangi but it was such a long time ago. I must have only been seven or eight.'

'That was when all the old kuia died – after the village was burnt. We have lots of tangi here. So many of our people die too young. You're lucky if you make it to sixty in this tribe.'

He glanced over their shoulders towards the car park. 'Ah, here's the mayor and the Minister of Maori Affairs. We'll be starting soon. When the women call you onto the marae with the karanga, keep your eyes lowered. It's a sign of respect. And take your shoes off before going inside the meeting house. Just follow the crowd and you'll be right.'

He shook hands with James and kissed both Shirley and Helene on the cheek. The fresh scent of shaving foam lingered. He strode over to greet the dignitaries as they stepped out of a sleek, silver Jaguar. Gusts of wind buffeted the umbrellas, which two burly security men were grappling to hold over the men of state. Helene was stunned. Mere had willingly weeded her garden, ironed her clothes and cleaned her house, and here she was being honoured at her funeral by the top politicians of the nation. She cringed at how she had so arrogantly misjudged this clearly influential woman.

'Can you believe it? Politicians at Mere's funeral!' James sounded almost excited.

'I can,' Shirley said. 'She was a judge of the Maori Land Court, and she did a lot of work with the Waitangi Tribunal. We talked about some of the cases when she visited. She was still working on one while she stayed with you two.'

'You never told us.' Helene tried to keep the accusation light.

'You never asked. And Mere liked to keep that side of her life quiet. She said it changed the way people treated her.'

A keening chant pierced the grey drizzle and silenced the crowd. A lone Maori woman, wearing a broad black hat and ankle length dress, stood in front of the meeting house calling the crowd of visitors onto the marae. It was eerie yet beautiful. The dignitaries, flanked by two Maori women, led the group through the carved archway. Helene, James and Shirley joined in near the back, taking small, slow steps, heads lowered and stopping with the crowd each time the women escorting the visitors sang their own chanting response. The lone Maori woman finished her chanting welcome, and a bare chested Maori warrior wearing a flax skirt and wielding a long carved stick advanced towards the visitors in what looked like a war dance.

'What's that stick he's holding?' Helene whispered to Shirley.

'It's a taiaha. They used it as a weapon in the old days. It takes years of practice to learn how to use it. Now it's mostly used for ceremonies, to challenge the visitors to see if they are friendly.'

The warrior looked terrifying. She could not take her eyes off him. She had never seen such a perfect physique. One thigh was heavily tattooed. She could imagine the ornate design extending up over his muscular buttocks beneath the tight black shorts. She glanced at James, who was also transfixed. He looked somehow taller, more alive than when he had left Brisbane. Her heart lurched at the thought of losing him. The subtle glances from the women around him and his relaxed, confident stance, which seemed so different to a few months ago, only worsened her fear that it was too late. Could she honestly expect him to have remained celibate for all these months, especially considering the shadow of doubt under which they had said goodbye? Her eyes focused on the half-naked warrior but her thoughts were on her husband.

The sombre crowd moved forward. All around her people were removing their damp shoes and placing them neatly each side of the main entrance, along with their dripping umbrellas. Everything was crying. She followed James and Shirley inside. There, to her right, was Mere's coffin surrounded by colourful wreaths of flowers and a large group of weeping women and children. Her heart lurched again, this time in grief. Mere's death hadn't seemed real until this moment. Tears sprang to her eyes. The worn, smooth floorboards caressed her bare feet. Both men and women were stopping briefly to acknowledge Mere, stooping to lay a wreath or to kiss or grasp the hand of one of the women. Shirley stopped. Her body trembled and she dabbed furiously at the tears with her lacy handkerchief. A graceful Maori woman around Shirley's age reached up and touched Shirley's hand.

'You're Shirley, aren't you? Thank you so much for coming.'

Shirley gave a tiny gasp of recognition.

'Tena koe, Arahia. After all these years …'

She bent over and kissed Arahia on her flawless brown cheek. It was the first time Helene had ever heard Shirley speak Maori. To her Australian ear the pronunciation sounded perfect.

They walked towards the back where the visitors had already filled five long rows of chairs. The dignitaries sat in the front row flanked by men. In fact, the front two rows held only men. Many of the women sat on the floor, lining the walls, including the two girls in their smart suits, their bare legs curled discretely underneath them. It was obviously not discreet enough, for she spotted the curt look of an old kuia who muttered something to her equally wizened neighbour. The neighbour pulled her faded tartan blanket off her lap and passed it along the line of sitting women. When it reached the two girls they knew exactly what was required. They uncurled their legs and covered the bare skin with the blanket. The old woman smiled a toothless smile, clearly relieved to have solved the problem.

They found three spare seats safely tucked at the edge of the back row. It was much warmer in here and surprisingly light and airy. Carved beams sloped high above her across the entire length of the building. The walls displayed more elaborate carvings. She could almost feel them looking at her.

Near the entrance, facing Mere and the grieving women, sat three rows of mostly older Maori men and women. Again the front row held men only. She nudged Shirley and nodded towards them.

'Who are they?'

'They are the elders of the tribe. The men who will speak sit in the front.'

'What about the women? Don't they have a say?'

'They are in charge of the karanga, the welcome and challenge as we walked on. Here, inside, their say is more subtle but equally as powerful. They lead the singing at the end of each speech as a sign of approval of the words spoken. The ultimate insult would be a refusal to sing – imagine it!' The clouds of grief parted for a brief moment and she smiled.

One of the elders in the front row stood up. The people instantly quietened. His commanding presence was as large as his stomach, which threatened to burst the seams of his suit jacket. His voice, as he started speaking in Maori, was rich and deep, like a barrel of honey. He spoke with his hands, gesturing to the carvings around the walls, to the visitors and to Mere's coffin.

The man finished his speech. 'Tena koutou, tena koutou, tena tatoa katoa.' He turned and nodded to the elders seated beside and behind him. They shuffled to their feet. Somewhere at the back a guitar strummed a muffled beat. Their voices soared, filling the meeting house with layers of harmony. Helene's chest constricted with emotion. It was beautiful.

Now it was the visitors' turn. A Maori man sitting next to the mayor stood up to speak. Again it was in Maori. He spoke with his hands and his feet, pacing a few steps back and forth. Everyone listened attentively and at one stage laughed at what must have been a joke. Helene wondered how many of them could understand. The speeches and songs went on for ages.

James squeezed her hand and smiled. She squeezed back.

Finally the speeches ended and the church service began. Each of Mere's grandchildren choked out a few words about their beloved nanny. Then Derek, flanked by his brothers and sisters, walked over to Mere's coffin and spoke directly to her. Tears welled in his eyes but his voice was steady and strong. Such oratory, such voices; like basking in warm sunshine they flowed over her, through her, melting and stirring her heart.

When the service finished they followed the crowd outside to watch six warrior-like men carry Mere's coffin to the waiting hearse. The rain had stopped and, as James had predicted, the sun was shining. The grandchildren placed the floral wreaths around her, tenderly patting the gleaming mahogany.

'Is the graveyard far away?' Helene asked.

'It's at the bottom of the hill. We can walk,' Shirley said.

It was exactly as Mere had described. Helene looked around at the cluster of neat, tidy buildings and across the grassy hillside, which sloped far away to a car park, gardens and a monument perched above the harbour. She tried to imagine Mere camping here during the protest, the tragic fire that had taken a little girl and the police dragging the people away. So much had happened here. They walked down the road past the old state houses, many now renovated but some still painted in their original blue.

To their left children were running, climbing and swinging at a large playground. They continued out to the main road, which snaked around the waterfront. A constant stream of cars and lycra-clad cyclists flowed past. Parked cars lined the road near the urupa and as one cyclist rode past a car door flung open. The cyclist swerved and yelled an obscenity. A woman dressed in a sleek, grey trouser suit, her fair hair caught up in a messy bun, stepped out and slammed the door. She reached the urupa entrance about the same time as James, Helene and Shirley.

'Damn cyclists. Far too many of them. No idea about road safety. Cars have doors so of course they are going to open.'

Her pale, freckled face creased when she spoke like the folds of an old map and her eyes shone out, bright blue and friendly.

'Sorry for the outburst. I'm not usually like that, at least not nowadays. Are you coming in? We had better hurry. I think we're the last.'

She flung a teary smile towards them and led the way into the urupa where Mere's family huddled together in little groups. Derek held the hand of a beautiful woman who kept pulling tissues out of her handbag like a magician and discreetly passing them to those around her. Mere's coffin lay poised over the grave, surrounded by flowers. While the minister and family spoke, Helene glanced around at the gravestones, reading the names and dates. This was no ordinary graveyard where complete strangers were buried side by side. In here the people were from the same tribe; they shared the same history. And from the ages on the headstones around her they did indeed seem to die young: kids, teenagers, a forty-three year old. Not one was over sixty.

The tall, pale woman standing next to Shirley blew her nose, dropped the sodden tissues into her orange handbag and patted Shirley's trembling arm. Tears streamed down Shirley's face.

'She was only our age. It's too young.'

'How did you know her?' asked the woman.

'We were childhood friends. We lived here until my family moved to Australia. We lost touch for many years but she came to visit only a few months ago. It was wonderful but …' she took a deep, ragged breath, 'it makes this so much harder.'

'Death is never easy, whichever way it happens.'

They were silent for a moment. Suddenly the woman gripped Shirley's arm. 'Oh! I know who you are. You're Shirley, the one who gave her the teddy bear.'

'Yes, that's me. She was heartbroken when he was burnt in the fire. I was too.'

The woman's bright eyes darted towards James. 'And you must be James. Mere really enjoyed your visits these past few months.'

'I did too. She really helped me sort out a few things.' His eye caught Helene's. 'I can't believe she's gone. She seemed fine last time I saw her.'

'She never was one to make a fuss. I'm Liz. We've been friends for … it must be close to thirty years now. Since law school. Lung cancer is a horrible way to go but she was so calm about it. Honestly, half the time she was the one comforting me.'

Shirley nodded. 'She was an amazing woman. I only wish we had caught up sooner.'

Liz patted her arm. 'But you did catch up. Think about that. There must have been a purpose.'

Four sombre men positioning themselves around Mere's coffin halted their whispered conversation. This was the worst part. The two women held hands. Helene moved closer to James. He put his arm around her waist. They watched in silence. She still couldn't believe it was Mere they were lowering into the ground. The coffin had hardly come to a rest when three brawny men in grubby overalls appeared with spades and started shovelling dirt into the hole. Muddy clods splattered the coffin with undignified thuds. What were they doing? Surely they should wait until everyone had gone? Yet Mere's family didn't look at all concerned. One of the men handed his spade to Derek. He took over the shovelling with a vengeance. All the sons and grandsons had a turn until the gaping hole became a smooth rectangle of fresh brown dirt. Derek patted the earth with the spade and then passed it, almost reverently, back to one of the waiting workers. He glanced at Helene, James and Shirley and then his gaze returned to Helene, more intently this time. What was he staring at? Helene self-consciously raised her hand to her chest. Her fingers touched Mere's greenstone pendant. Derek just stared.

34

'Mind if I sit here?' Derek squeezed into the empty chair beside Shirley, opposite James and Helene. Shirley, oblivious to Derek's arrival, kept chatting to her generously proportioned neighbour who was digging into a huge plate of trifle and whipped cream. Derek set his cup of tea down and took a thick slice of banana cake from a large platter. Every table in the communal dining hall heaved with food and people, talking and laughing. The few funerals she had attended had been far more subdued affairs. Helene chased the last of the peas around her plate, finishing them off with a final mouthful of the most delicious baked salmon she had tasted.

'Have you had enough to eat?' Derek asked, licking icing off his fingers.

James pushed away his empty dessert bowl. 'What a feast. Thanks, mate.'

'Don't thank me. It's the ladies who do all the work. They always put on a good feed, don't you, Lucy?'

Lucy, her jam roll figure squashed into a white apron, whisked up the dirty plates and grinned a gummy smile.

'It keeps us out of mischief, ay? Cup of tea, anyone?'

'I'd love one, thanks,' said Helene.

'Righto. I'll bring over the teapot.' She waddled away.

Derek brushed some cake crumbs off his grey silk tie. 'We always finish a tangi with a meal. It breaks the tapu, the sacredness, so we can return to the living. We never send our visitors away without feeding them up. Hospitality is very important in Maori culture.'

'It's wonderful,' said Helene. 'I've never experienced anything like it.'

Derek's gaze flicked to the greenstone pendant. He cleared his throat.

'Actually I came over to ask you about your hei matau, the fishing hook. Where did you get it?'

Helene touched the smooth greenstone in an almost protective gesture. Should she have worn it? Was Derek angry? He must recognise it as his mum's.

'Your mum gave it to me when she came over to stay with us to finish her book.'

'I thought so.' Derek rubbed his chin and stared at the green stone.

'Would you like it?' Helene started to pull the black cord over her head. 'I know it is very special to your family. I didn't want to take it but she insisted.'

'No, no. You must keep it. Mum never did anything without good reason. Did she say why she wanted you to have it?'

'She said something about praying and feeling that I should have it.'

Derek relaxed back in his chair and grinned. 'Yep, that's Mum all right. She never made a big deal about it but when she got one of those feelings, nothing could sway her. Like going to Australia to finish her book. It didn't make sense. We all tried to persuade her to stay. People had offered her their holiday houses on Waiheke Island and up the coast but she insisted on going. Perhaps you were the reason.'

Lucy returned lugging an enormous metal teapot. She poured the hot, strong brew into the cups, leaning close to Helene.

'There you go, luvvy.' Her face was like a plump, ripe plum and her breathing puffed like an old steam train.

'Thank you.' Helene watched her shuffle to the next table, her swollen legs protruding from her floral dress like a couple of tree stumps.

James reached for a slice of cake. 'Mere seemed happy with what she had done on her book when I last saw her. Did she finish it? Have you read it?'

'Yes, she finished it just last week. Stubborn old mule, she was. Do you know I caught her typing on her laptop in her hospital bed? The nurses gave her a good telling off. We were all amazed that she had the strength. Now I'm glad she ignored us all. The parts I've read, well, it's as though I'm right there with her.'

'What a wonderful gift for your family.'

'Mum was always thinking about others, right to the end. That was part of her problem. She never looked after herself. We had been nagging her for ages to get that cough checked out. By the time she did, it was too late.'

'She was like that with us too – so kind. She was never too busy to stop and talk.' Helene sighed. 'Despite the short time I knew her, I really miss her. I can't imagine how it must be for you.'

Derek touched a finger to his eye smearing away an errant tear.

'Do you know the best part of the whole tangi was when we put the dirt on her coffin. It was as though I was tucking her in, keeping her safe. You know, only three of her generation have made it to sixty. All the rest died younger. Some of them reckon it's from eating all that kai from the polluted bay when they were kids.'

'Is it still polluted?' James asked.

'Not since they shut down the sewerage outlet.'

'They let sewerage straight into the bay down there? That's disgusting.'

'We're not the only tribe who had to deal with stuff like that. Our old people throughout the country have similar stories. But Mum and Dad were never ones to get stuck on the past. They always said it was important to reveal the truth, to tell the stories that so few people know about, to obtain some sort of justice, and then to move forward. That's what Mum tried to do with her work.'

'So where is this tribe up to in the process?' James leaned forward clearly intrigued.

'After years of protests and petitions we have finally regained some of our ancestral land and received financial compensation for

175

what cannot be returned. Mum was instrumental in getting the final settlement sorted. The negotiations have taken years, what with the change of government and things. It only happened a few weeks ago. I'm just glad she lived long enough to see it.'

'What did the settlement give you? Are you happy with it?' asked James.

'We're more relieved than happy. No amount of money can ever repay what was taken from us. We wouldn't expect that, anyway. It's not just about the money; the land has spiritual significance for us. The return of our whenua, our land, is the first step to regaining our self-esteem as a people. Now our focus is on education, housing and health. We offer grants for our young people to study at university. More and more are getting degrees – lawyers, doctors, teachers.'

'And they come back here to help the tribe?' Helene asked.

Derek laughed. 'Hardly. They head overseas where they can earn better money.'

Helene thought about Lucy with her puffy face and swollen legs. 'What about health?'

'We have three health clinics. One is just over the road there.' He gestured behind him. 'Our doctors are fantastic but we desperately need more.'

James nudged her. She threw him a warning frown. She already had a good job, thank you.

Derek continued. 'We have more than our fair share of health problems. Despite the improvements we still have a long way to go.'

Helene watched Lucy scoop up a little girl wearing a baggy, faded pink dress and smack a big kiss on her cheek. The child flung her arms around her neck and kissed her back, then wriggled free and raced outside.

It was those squirming little bare feet that did it. She'd seen them before; not exactly the same legs but close enough. Squirming, brown bare feet sticking out from an oversized floral dress and her granddad's gentle bear hands tickling the soles, making her giggle while he inspected her crater-scarred legs.

'See this, Helene?' He'd turned to her, inviting her to step closer. 'This poor wee tot has chronic scabies. It leaves terrible scars but is so easily fixed with a good dose of antibiotics.' He smiled and spoke to the child's mother in a language Helene didn't understand. Helene could not tear her eyes from the child's ravaged legs. 'Have you got those bananas?' Granddad asked. She nodded, pulled a cluster from the box and handed them to her granddad, who passed them on to the Aboriginal woman. 'Some silly white do-gooder made them rip out all the bananas around here. Said it attracted the snakes.' Granddad snorted. 'The snakes aren't the problem.'

How could she have forgotten the sadness, the elation, the compassion that surged through her eleven-year-old mind that day? She could still see the snuffling kids smearing away sluggish streams of thick green snot. 'Ear infection,' her granddad would mutter. 'It's too late for this lad. Wrecked his hearing.' His big bear hands measured out a dose of thick, red syrup. He passed it to the boy and patted him on the back like a father would his son. Flying home that evening across the vast outback desert, his big bear hands wrapped around a water flask that smelt like whiskey, Granddad had said, 'Us white fellas handing out medicine and fruit won't solve the problem but at least it's something.' Granddad had lived, and died, for his work.

A loud crash and a shout snapped Helene back to the present. All heads spun towards the kitchen as a panicked dishwasher, still holding her tea-towel rushed out.

'Someone call a doctor. Lucy's collapsed!'

Helene hurried into the kitchen, closely followed by James and Derek. Lucy lay stranded in a sea of pots and smashed plates. Someone already had the broom out, clearing a path through the debris, while a teenage girl knelt at Lucy's side shaking and patting her in an attempt to rouse her. Helene knelt on the floor next to her.

'I'm a doctor,' she said as she felt for a pulse. Weak and rapid but still there. Breathing – laboured. Hands – cold and clammy. She glanced up at the anxious crowd hovering around them.

'Could someone call an ambulance? She needs to get to hospital as soon as possible.'

Just at that moment Lucy's eyes opened wide. She snatched her hand away from Helene's.

'No! No hospital. No Pakeha doctors.'

Derek dropped to his knees beside her.

'Lucy, this isn't the time to argue. You need to get to the hospital.'

Lucy rolled her head from side to side, a look of wild panic in her eyes. 'No, no. I won't go. I just need a cup of tea.' She tried to sit up but slumped back, squeezing her eyes shut like a child playing hide and seek.

Helene leaned over her trying to soothe her. 'It will be all right, I promise. The doctors will help you.' Lucy's eyes flickered open. Helene didn't notice that the greenstone pendant had slipped out of her dress until she heard Lucy gasp and saw her startled eyes spring wide open, her pudgy fingers straining to touch it.

'It's you. The one in the prophecy. You've come to help us.'

35

Helene stood with Derek and James, watching the ambulance, with Lucy safely on board, exit the car park. 'What prophecy? What was Lucy talking about?' she asked Derek.

As soon as Lucy had seen the pendant her breathing had settled. She had even smiled when the orderlies helped her onto a stretcher and carted her off to the ambulance. Derek pushed the wayward lock of hair off his face. 'Come. Let's sit over here.'

They followed him to a wooden bench positioned to take in the full panorama of the harbour and islands now basking in warm sunlight.

'In 1780, our ancestor, Tītahi, stood here on this point and saw a vision of three nautilus shells coming up the harbour. They represented the coming of the British. He foretold how they would bring both good and bad to our people. We have suffered great injustice at the hands of the Pakeha but over the years, at certain times, there have been Pakeha who have brought great good. Some of the old people, including Lucy, believe that this is a part of the prophecy that continues today. In times of great need when we cannot provide for ourselves the prophecy, or whoever inspired the prophecy, sends the right person to help us. Back in the 1930s when our tribe needed help with land rights there was Judge Acheson. In the fifties when our kids needed spiritual direction there was the minister who used to drive around every Sunday and pick them all up in his beat up red station wagon and take them down to church. In the seventies people from all over the world came to support us in our stand here on Bastion Point. Only a few weeks ago we finally settled the land issue. Now one of our main needs is health.'

'I'm not that person. I can't be. I know nothing about the Maori people.'

Derek rubbed his chin. 'Perhaps not. Lucy can be rather dramatic about these things.'

'But what if you are?' James said.

'You mean you believe it?' She had never thought of James as the superstitious type. Perhaps his visits with Mere had something to do with it.

'Why not? I saw how Lucy changed the moment she touched the pendant.'

'You know half the problem with our people is that they don't get medical help when they should, often out of fear,' said Derek.

'But I'm not Maori.'

'True, but you wear the pounamu.' Derek reached out and touched it. 'This one is more than jewellery, you know.'

Emotion welled up within her. What was this? Grief for Mere, yes, but more than that. Her heart ached for the whole tribe. And there was something else: a sense of peace and … she struggled to identify it.

James took her hand. 'Maybe you should read Mere's stories?' He looked at Derek. 'That is, if it's okay with you?'

'Absolutely. Perhaps you will feel—as I did—that she's right there talking to you.'

36

MERE

'Mere, are you ready to go?'

Arahia tapped on my bedroom door. I glanced once more at the words from Isaiah: *Those who hope in the Lord will renew their strength. They will run and not grow weary, they will walk and not be faint.*

Yes, on this momentous day strength was exactly what I needed. The cancer had curled its tentacles through my lungs, suffocating more and more of the healthy tissue. Whenever I walked more than a few steps they would clench in protest, stifling the remaining trickle of air. The wheelchair and oxygen bottle sat quietly in the corner – on loan from the hospital. They could stay there today. I would not have their hampering presence distracting people from the ceremony. I closed the Bible on my lap and patted the cover.

'So Lord, I can do all things with you who strengthens me. Can you give me a hand up off this bed?'

I felt a familiar warmth through my frail arms and pushed myself up onto my feet.

'Thanks.'

My conversations with the Lord were more frequent and more real than they had ever been. As my time here on this earth drew to a close it was as if I already had a foot in the next world, straddling the two. No one seemed to mind. Death brought with it a tolerance for the spiritual even from those who doubted.

Arahia tapped at the door again, then poked her head around the corner.

'Do you need help?'

'No, no, I'm all ready to go.'

I picked up my bag and brushed an imaginary speck of dirt off my white coat.

Arahia swept into the room, all efficient even without her matron's uniform.

'Liz has just arrived. You go on ahead with her and I'll bring the wheelchair.'

I shook my head. 'No, not today.'

Arahia opened and closed her mouth like a fish, biting back the telling off she wanted to give me. 'Well at least take the oxygen, just in case.'

'I'm not having that either.'

She shook her head in exasperation, then laughed. 'You stubborn old woman. I'm putting it in the boot anyway.'

Her teasing punch on my arm revived fond childhood memories although it had usually been me doing the punching back then. It was so good spending these last few weeks in her home. She clucked around me like an old chook, enticing me to eat her homemade chicken soup and chatting non-stop.

The front door opened and Liz whirled in, all smiles and orange nail polish.

'What a great morning – a bit cold but no rain, thank goodness. Ooh, you look fantastic in that coat! Where did you get it?'

'It was Mum's. She only wore it on special occasions. If she was here she would wear it today.'

'She certainly would. It will be just as though she's there with us.'

Liz kissed my sunken cheek and took my elbow. 'Come on then. We don't want to miss out on a car park. See you there, Arahia!'

Arahia came down the hall lugging the oxygen bottle. 'Hold on a moment. You need to take this.'

'It keeps her happy,' I whispered to Liz.

Arahia wagged her finger at me like a scolding mother. 'I heard that. Liz, don't you let her fool you with that "I'm all right" story.'

'No worries there. I've had years of practice, haven't I?' She laughed and patted my arm. I smiled. Laughing would set off a coughing fit, which would only make them fuss more.

Sunlight streamed into the car, making my eyes heavy. I rested my head back and allowed them to close. It was Saturday the fifth of November. My mokopuna would be buying fireworks to let off tonight with their friends. On this very day in 1881 more than two thousand villagers of Parihaka, in the Taranaki region, had greeted sixteen hundred armed police troops, not with guns but with songs, bread and peace. Such bravery, such self-control. The leaders were arrested, the village destroyed and the people dispersed. We didn't need to celebrate a failed attempt to blow up parliament on the other side of the world. Parihaka, and this day too, were far greater causes for remembrance and celebration. A gentle shaking roused me.

'Mere, we're here.'

'Already?' I looked out the window. We were parked on Tamaki Drive right outside the urupa. Across the road boats bobbed at their anchors and kayakers skimmed over the smooth water. A lone swimmer in the water reminded me of the night long ago when I had set fire to Liz's dad's boat. Now she sat beside me, my closest friend, gently waking me.

Next to the urupa, on the grassy reserve, about where Uncle Wiri's house had been, was an enormous marquee erected over a long table set up with the official documents. It wasn't far to walk but it still felt as though I was wading through the mudflats as we used to when we wanted a feed of flounder. Liz discreetly held my arm and chatted away as though it was the most normal thing in the world to take so long to walk such a short distance.

We sat in the front row. A good third of our people had turned up. They filled the rows of white plastic chairs and stood around the perimeter, chatting or dragging a final few puffs of nicotine before the formalities began. Pot plants and the deep red carved statues of our ancestors delineated the official area. Four ministers of the Crown sat behind the podium in their spit polished shoes. Our elders sat with them, wearing the feather coats of their ancestors. It was a regal scene: one to be imprinted on the memory of every member of our tribe. I sighed.

Liz leant over, looking worried. 'Should I get the oxygen? Are you all right?'

I patted her knee. 'Couldn't be better.'

'It's not every day you see a government saying sorry, as we well know.'

'Ai.' I nodded in agreement. From our first taste of land law almost twenty years earlier we had both fought for the legal rights of the dispossessed. My heart was for my own people but Liz had travelled the world in her typically free-spirited zeal for justice.

The formalities started. Our young men looked magnificent wielding the taiaha and wearing their red armbands – a memorial to the people who had lost their lands. Finally, the Minister for the Treaty of Waitangi Negotiations took the microphone.

'Ngati Whatua Orakei lost virtually all their lands as a result of the past actions of the Crown and now is the time to right the wrongs of the past. This settlement breathes new life into the relationship between Ngati Whatua and the Crown, and will bring benefit to all the people of Auckland.'

I patted a stray tear from the corner of my eye. Behind me, I heard teary sniffs as others allowed this formal apology to unlock the grief so long pent up in their hearts. One of our elders rose to respond. He spoke with a dignity born of the pain and freedom of forgiveness.

'This is a day of celebration without recriminations, a day of healing, a day for Ngati Whatua to cry tears of joy, a day for reconstruction not retribution, a day to build a new future for our grandkids.'

He turned to speak directly to the minister. 'Today you have redeemed the Crown in the eyes of God. Where you sit, sir, is where Tumutumuwhenua, our ancestral house, was torched. Behind you is the urupa where our grief stricken people are buried.'

You can forgive but you never forget. At that moment I saw again the flames of our village, I felt their fierce heat and murderous crackle. I heard the old kuia wailing. I felt my koro's arms around me and I saw his tears through my own. I turned my head towards the beach. I saw Rewiti and his mates swimming and laughing. Then I saw him dying on his bed, gasping for breath as the typhoid stole him away from us. I closed my eyes. A single tear rolled down my cheek. Liz squeezed my hand. I saw the flames of her dad's boat and then I saw the deadly flames that had stolen a little girl's life. I looked at that little girl's father sitting there amongst the elders, accepting the government's apology with a grace that some of our younger people struggled with. Age mellows the warrior and magnifies wisdom. Both youth and age are necessary.

The speeches finished. The dignitaries solemnly filed along the table, signing the documents to ratify the settlement that returned to us sixteen million dollars along with the title to Pourewa Creek and the right to buy back three point two hectares of land on the North Shore directly across the harbour from where we now sat. We never would - never could - demand the more than thirty thousand hectares our tribe had lost. This settlement returned to us more than land or money, it returned our mana.

More than one hundred of us followed the dignitaries. When it was my turn I picked up the pen and signed my name.

This is for you Nanny, Granddad, Mum, Dad and Rewiti. I have lived to see this day and I am signing this on your behalf.

I looked towards the urupa, half expecting them to be standing there applauding. Of course they weren't there. The tentacles squeezed my lungs and I bent over in a spasm of coughing. I would see them soon enough.

The prophecy of my ancestor, Titahi, as he stood on the headland of Takaparawhau and surveyed his tribe's land spread out below him in every direction.

What is this wind that blows
Rattling around me,
'Tis the North wind

185

Bringing the nautilus shells ashore
Bringing a new people, new ideas, a new order.
There is another wind I feel rising from the south, a cold wind
The carved post rises on the shores of the Waitemata
A symbol of authority and power (beware of it)
Good will eventually come to Tamaki Makaurau
Ah … my vision is that of peace.

The north wind did indeed bring the British in their ships shaped like nautilus shells. At our invitation, they sailed up the Waitemata Harbour and settled here in Tamaki Makaurau, also known as Auckland. We embraced the good they brought and in turn gave them our most valued possession: land. But greed and the lust for power decimated our land and our people. Titahi saw smoke rising from the carved post – the fires of destruction. I too, in my grief and anger, added to that smoke. No race is better than another; we are all human, capable of great evil and great good. Today I have seen the fulfilment of this prophecy. My vision is that of peace …

37

HELENE

Helene closed the simply bound book. She had been sitting here on Bastion Point all afternoon reading Mere's stories. They read like fiction yet they were true. The words swirled in her mind like the early evening mist that gathered over Rangitoto Island. She could make out vague shapes of meaning but not quite grasp them. That prophecy was so beautiful but could it really apply to her? She needed Mere's guidance. She stood up and stretched. The damp grass chilled her bare feet. It felt good. She rubbed the pounamu that nestled cool and still against her skin. What was it Mere had said? It wasn't the stone that gave peace but the maker of the stone. Mere would have prayed. She took a deep breath and spoke into the crisp evening breeze.

'What does it mean? What should I do?'

The sun hung low behind the bridge, spilling its last orange hues across the harbour. Perhaps Titahi had stood in this exact spot when he saw his vision. She stared across the water, conjuring images of nautilus shells sailing into view. No wonder the government had tried to get this land. A house here would be amazing. But then she wouldn't be standing in this peaceful reserve, freely open for all to enjoy. These Maori people, renowned as mighty warriors, were also generous. The same wave of peace she had felt as Derek spoke to her returned. And something else. What was it? The swirling mist formed a single word: purpose. She knew what she had to do.

Clutching Mere's book she walked back up to the marae and Derek's office. She knocked tentatively at his door, surprised that he was still there at this late hour.

'Come in, come in,' he welcomed her. 'Sit down for a moment and tell me what you thought of it.' He touched the book almost reverently as she placed it on the desk between them.

'It was just as you said; as though she was there with me.'

He nodded and pressed his fingers to his lips thoughtfully, waiting for her to continue.

'I … I really think …' The certainty of a few minutes before left her with a swiftness that stole her voice. Another voice bombarded her mind: *Don't do it. This place isn't for you. You'll lose everything.*

She looked down, twisting her fingers in her lap.

Derek spoke quietly. 'Since that little drama with Lucy yesterday I have had time to think.'

Helene interrupted. 'How is Lucy? Have you heard from the hospital?'

'I spoke to her daughter today. She's fighting fit, fighting being the operative word. They want to monitor her for a few days but they'll be lucky to keep her in that long. She sneaked out this morning and tried to hail a taxi. One of the ward nurses who had just come off her shift recognised her. I think the pink fluffy slippers gave her away.'

Helene smiled. 'They do every time. Anyway it's a good thing that the hospital is sorting her out.'

'It will be a first for her. She's one of a handful of our people who are still wary of modern medicine,' he tapped his designer glasses 'unlike the rest of us. I don't know if she has ever seen a doctor.'

'She should be having regular check-ups.'

'She might if you worked here.' He raised his hands in front of him and grinned. 'No pressure, of course. You know, I have always believed in my ancestor's prophecy. I also believe that Mum would not have given you that pounamu without good reason. However, whether you believe in the prophecy or not, you still have free choice. We could sure do with your skills, Helene, but not unless you truly want to give them.'

She braced her hands on the chair and leaned forward. 'Half an hour ago I knew it was the right thing to do. I really felt it. Now I'm wondering if it's all the emotion of the past few days.' She exhaled back and crossed her arms in front of her.

Derek gave her a generous smile. 'You need to be certain. Take your time. Go off with James tomorrow and think about it. We'll still be here when you get back.'

38

'Now will you tell me where are we going?' Helene watched the airport parking machine swallow their ticket as rapidly as they had gulped their tea and toast at some inhumane hour this morning. Shirley was on the early flight to Brisbane, anxious to whip up her famous lamingtons and pineapple cake for tomorrow's Country Women's Institute fundraiser. 'You promised you would tell me as soon as your mum left.'

The exit barrier rose and James merged into the minimal airport traffic, in no hurry to illuminate her. 'Patience, patience. She won't have even boarded the plane yet.'

Helene groaned. 'Can't you just give me a clue, please?' Pleading would get her nowhere but it was fun. She poked him in the ribs. She had forgotten how ticklish he was. His sudden jerk made the car swerve.

'Careful, you'll make me hit a sheep.'

Indeed there were sheep grazing in the lush, green paddocks alongside the road. A jumbo jet, nose up, wheels down, roared into land barely metres above them. Oblivious to the giant machine, the sheep contentedly nibbled their grassy breakfast. The rural road soon became a highway with large green signs indicating 'south'.

'So we're heading south. How far?' James stole an amused glance. 'I'm not telling you anything. It's a surprise. Just sit back and enjoy the scenery.'

There was plenty of scenery to enjoy. New Zealand was not only renowned for its sheep. They drove up over the Bombay Hills against the early morning traffic as it sped towards the city. Ploughed fields of rich, terracotta red earth undulated across the hills that marked the southern border of Auckland. Fog shrouded the plain below. James switched on the lights as they descended into the gloom.

'It will soon lift.' He spoke like an enthusiastic tour guide, pointing out places of interest as they meandered over rolling hills and across the lush, green farmland of the Waikato. A cloudless blue sky soon spread above them, pouring sunlight through the window.

This was their third day together but their first chance to really talk. They had been so busy, first with Mere's tangi and then with Shirley. James had spent yesterday escorting his mum on a reminiscent tour of her childhood haunts after dropping Helene at Bastion Point to read Mere's stories.

They drove through the main street of a small farming town. Quaint churches, cafes and antique shops lined each side. Just out of town, past farm machinery and tractor yards, they turned onto the highway signposted to Rotorua. She had heard of it from Lloyd: a steamy city full of bubbling hot mud pools and a spectacular geyser that spurted boiling water metres into the air every half hour. She rubbed the pendant, cool and soothing. Speaking her thoughts out loud was scary; a commitment, no turning back. She took a deep breath and blurted out the words.

'I know this sounds bizarre but I really think that I am meant to help those people.'

James didn't answer immediately. They were speeding past a queue of cars backed up behind a Mercedes pulling a horse float. It turned up a long driveway flanked by white post and rail fences bordering immaculately groomed paddocks holding a dozen sleek horses.

Once they were safely past with a clear road ahead he replied. 'It's not so bizarre. When we first met you used to talk about wanting to help others the way your granddad did. I know it's not exactly the flying doctor, but as Derek said, his people do need help.'

Again she pictured the little girl's squirming brown legs beneath the faded, baggy dress. She remembered her trusting smile. 'But it's crazy. I would have to give up my career in Brisbane, break my deal with Russell and take a major pay cut. It's career sabotage.'

'And you would have to swap your Oroton bag for one of those flax baskets.'

'I'm serious, you know.'

His voice lowered. 'I am too. Moving here would be good for us.'

Us. The word was like a choice morsel of food feeding a part of her heart she hadn't realised was so hungry. Despite the weeks apart, he spoke as though they were a team. Could he really have remained faithful? She hardly deserved it after the way she had treated him. Her eyes started to burn. She blinked back the tears. She reached across and squeezed his hand as it rested on his thigh.

'I'm so sorry about everything. I'm glad you've found a job you love. You deserve it. You've worked so hard and you're a great designer. I'm proud of you.'

He didn't say anything, just squeezed her hand back and shifted in his seat. It could have been her imagination but somehow he seemed to sit straighter, taller.

The rolling farmland gave way to steeper, rugged paddocks as they wound up over the ranges towards Rotorua. Strange rock formations littered the rough farmland creating a moon-like landscape. The terrain levelled out and in the distance below them Helene spotted a lake. 'That must be Lake Rotorua. Lloyd brought his management team over here last year to do some luxury hunting and fishing resort. We're not going fishing, are we?'

'No fishing and no hunting, but I bet we'll be keen to try out the hot pools later.'

At a small T-junction he turned left, away from the signs for the city. 'Not far now.'

She caught his excitement. The road wound around the edge of the lake past sparsely scattered houses and more sheep. They finally turned onto a highway running down the other side of the lake. Before she could ask where on earth they were going James turned into a gravel car park in front of a cute purple and yellow building splattered with bright signs. A minivan laden with yellow rafts was parked at the side.

'White water rafting! I've always wanted to do this!'

'I knew you would like it.' His expression transported her back to their first few years together: his delight in surprising her with some new adventure and her delight at being surprised. She looked at him, momentarily serious. 'Thank you.'

They jumped out of the car. Helene was opening the boot to grab their swimming gear when she felt a strong hand catch her arm.

'Leave that a moment.' James spun her around, and pulled her towards him. He held her close and kissed her, not the usual passionless peck but one full of longing. The years peeled away. Long forgotten sensations burst upon her, surprising her with their intensity. No pretending, no resistance, she pressed her body into his and tasted the trace of toothpaste still on his tongue. It was better than she remembered. They finally pulled apart.

James was grinning in that old larrikin way. 'So let's do this thing!'

Life jackets, t-shirts, sun hats and other tourist paraphernalia hung from racks around the shop. A large television showed rafts careening through turbulent white water. The lady behind the desk registered their booking and directed them to a large room lined with plastic chairs, a water cooler, coffee machine and another television fixed high in one corner. They waited, smiling at a middle aged couple chatting in German, their teenage kids tuned more into their iPods than their parents. James immediately fixated on the television – rugby of course. Helene picked up a magazine and flicked through the pages. A photo of a military gravestone halted her hapless browsing. It filled the page. The story squeezed in around it told of a New Zealand military doctor killed by a grenade blast while tending to a wounded soldier. The gravestone was pristinely white – a slab of the finest Italian marble standing to attention in an emerald expanse of militarily manicured lawn. It was not so much the gravestone as the epitaph engraved upon it that jumped out from the page, as though highlighted in bold.

Greater love has no one than this, that he lay down his life for his friends.

The young doctor's face, inset in the corner of the page, smiled out, full of youthful promise. He hadn't intended to die and yet he had, just like her granddad. What a waste of skills, of talent, of life. She sighed and slumped a little in her seat. Then it struck her: these men hadn't laid down their life at the moment they died; they had done it years earlier. The plane crash hadn't stolen her granddad's life; he had willingly laid it down when he had chosen to help those desperately remote communities over the lure of academic accolades and financial fortune. He had laid down one type of life, true, but he had gained another type of life, one full of adventure and contentment. Now James was asking her to lay down her life, her job, to move here. Was it really such a sacrifice? She glanced at James, still engrossed in the rugby game, and gave a wry smile. A giant set of scales descended in her mind. On one side were James, New Zealand and the little Maori girl with the scarred legs. On the other side: her full diary and her empty house. This was not how she had planned her life and yet …

'Hey, everyone. Welcome to River Rats.' The rafting guide leaned on the back of a chair at the front of the room. His messy hair hung in damp waves around his face.

'Are you all ready for a fantastic ride? There's heaps of water running today so it will be pretty exciting.' He flashed a practiced smile at the expectant group and continued. 'The highlight of this particular river is the seven metre waterfall. We're all up for that, yeah?' He gave the thumbs up and returned the enthusiastic nods.

Helene whispered to James. 'Did he say seven metres?'

He grinned. 'The highest commercially rafted waterfall in the world, according to the brochure. You're not scared, are you?' It was his teasing voice, baiting her with the challenge.

After the obligatory safety briefing, they donned wetsuits and life jackets and boarded the minivan for the short ride to their starting point. The guides bounced the bright yellow rafts off the bus, sliding them down the grassy bank into the river. James and

194

Helene clambered onto the raft, taking their assigned positions, along with the German family. The guide pushed off and a gentle current propelled them towards the first set of rapids. Following the guide's shouted commands, they manoeuvred through, spinning the raft to the left and then the right, straining backwards and then powering forwards. It was all over quickly and they rested their paddles as the river smoothed out into a deeply shaded canyon. Steep banks thick with native bush rose on either side. Why did it look familiar? A ray of sunlight, momentarily breaking through the trees on the ridge, flashed off her wedding ring. She had worn it for three weeks now without eczema. Was that significant? A psychosomatic sign?

The guide's lazy drawl caught her attention. James was asking him a question.

'Do you plan how you'll get through the rapids or is it gut instinct?'

'A bit of both, mate. Mostly it's about keeping your eyes on where you want to end up and going for it. If you focus on the rocks, you'll hit them.'

James caught her eye. 'Sounds like a good philosophy for life.' Before she could reply his attention shot back to the guide who was recounting his recent adventures rafting the Zambezi to the enraptured German teenagers. She looked at the deep green foliage looming above her. Still, silent, strangely familiar. James was right. She should be looking at where she wanted to end up. Steve had teased her about marriage and mercy. When she really thought about it, wasn't that what she had always wanted: a good relationship and the chance to help people? She had spent so much time dwelling on the problems in their marriage that she had almost singlehandedly sunk it.

High above her a woman emerged from the shadows, a Maori woman. Mere! She smiled and reached out her hand. Was this real or was this her dream? The woman in her dream had reached out her hand to help just as Mere had helped her in real life. Helene closed her eyes and shook her head. When she reopened her eyes the woman was still there but waving to a child who skipped into view along a track that ran through the bush. Of course it wasn't Mere.

'Forward paddle!' The guide's curt directive snapped her back to reality. The gentle river was no more. The raft lurched through the white water. The wild current spun it backwards, forcing it between two large rocks. Everyone paddled furiously. The guide yelled orders. They smashed into the bank and bounced off, bobbing in smooth water again but only for a moment. She heard the roar before she saw it. The river abruptly ended just a few metres ahead.

'Get down and hang on,' the guide yelled. They crouched low in the raft, tucking their legs in tight, chins down, holding their paddles flat against the raft.

A random thought, like a last minute deal, reverberated through her mind.

If the raft stays upright, everything will be all right.

The raft plummeted over the waterfall. Her head snapped backwards. Water rushed up her nose. For a moment all was black. Her arms and legs flailed in the deep water. Which way was up? Suddenly a strong hand reached out and grabbed her, pulling her to the surface. She gulped in precious air. The German family, jovially slapping each other on their life jackets, bobbed near the rebel raft waiting for the guide to flip it upright.

James held her tightly. 'I've got you, Helene. Everything will be all right.'

Her lungs burned. Her nose smarted. A wave of exhilaration and relief rippled through her, tugging at the corners of her mouth. She wrapped her arms around his neck and kissed him. Yes, everything would be all right.

High on the track above them a Maori woman looked down and smiled.

Glossary

E hoa	term of address to a friend
E kui	term of address to an old lady
E moko	term of address to a grandchild, shortened form of mokopuna.
Haka	fierce, rhythmical dance
Harekeke	flax leaf–Phormium tenax
Hikoi	march
Hui	meeting
Kai	food
Kaimoana	seafood
Karakia	prayer
Kaumatua	old man or elder
Kete	bag or basket
Koro	grandfather
Kuia	old lady
Kumara	sweet potato
Mana	spiritual status and influence infused with dignity and humility
Manuhiri	visitors
Marae	meeting house, the central building or area of a village
Matua	uncle, respectful term for older man
Mokopuna	grandchild
Tangi	funeral
Tena koe/koutou	greeting, welcome
Tohunga	expert, in this case an expert in Maori medicine and spirituality
Waka	canoe
Whaea	aunty, respectful term for older lady
Whanau	family
Whare	house
Whenua	land
Wharenui	carved meeting house
Upoko kohua	vehement swear word
Urupa	cemetery